# SUPERDOG!

## JENNY DALE

Illustrations by Mick Reid
Cover illustration by Michael Rowe

---

AN
**APPLE**
PAPERBACK

---

SCHOLASTIC INC.
New York  Toronto  London  Auckland  Sydney
Mexico City  New Delhi  Hong Kong  Buenos Aires

**SPECIAL THANKS TO VINCE CROSS**

No part of this publication may be reproduced in whole or in part, or stored in a retrieval system, or transmitted in any form or by any means, electronic, mechanical, photocopying, recording, or otherwise, without written permission of the publisher. For information regarding permission, write to Macmillan Publishers Ltd., 20 New Wharf Rd., London N1 9RR Basingstoke and Oxford.

ISBN 0-439-38921-6

Text copyright © 2003 by Working Partners Limited.
Illustrations copyright © 2003 by Mick Reid.

All rights reserved. Published by Scholastic Inc., 557 Broadway, New York, NY 10012 by arrangement with Macmillan Children's Books, a division of Macmillan Publishers Ltd.

SCHOLASTIC and associated logos are trademarks and/or registered trademarks of Scholastic Inc.

12 11 10 9 8 7 6 5 4 3 2          3 4 5 6 7 8/0

Printed in the U.S.A.          40
First Scholastic printing, February 2003

# CHAPTER ONE

"There's Blackpool Tower," said Neil Parker, his nose pressed against the vibrating train window. "It's just like the Eiffel Tower in Paris." As he spoke, the Manchester Express bounced over a bump and Neil's nose hit the glass hard. "Ow!" he exclaimed.

Neil's younger sister, Emily, giggled. "I hope there's time for us to go to the top," she said. "I bet the view's amazing. You can probably see King Street Kennels from up there!"

"Don't be silly," said Neil. "It's big, but not as high as all that. Anyway, I'm not sure Jake's got a head for heights. Do you, Jake?"

Jake, Neil's eight-month-old black-and-white Border collie puppy, stirred for a moment on Emily's lap.

1

She stroked his ears tenderly. Jake snuffled and then settled again.

"Jake's been terrific," said Emily. "He's coped so well with the trip."

Neil nodded. "Dad gave him something to make sure he wasn't anxious on the train. I can't remember what it was called. *Super*-something."

"Well, it's certainly worked." Emily smiled. "I've never seen him so quiet."

"Dad said it was a mild tranquilizer and that he wouldn't give him much, anyway," Neil went on knowledgeably. "Even short journeys in the car sometimes get him too excited. Jake'll be back to normal in no time. You'll see."

Bob and Carole Parker, Neil and Emily's parents, ran King Street Kennels and rescue center in the small town of Compton. All the family loved dogs, even Sarah, Neil and Emily's five-year-old sister. And there were a lot of dogs to love at King Street.

"I hope Sam's going to be all right at home without us." Neil sounded wistful for a moment and looked out of the window again.

"Of course he will. Nothing'll happen to him while we're away." Emily tried to sound reassuring. "And anyway, we'll see Dad on Sunday and we can ask about him when he comes to pick us up. Don't worry!"

Sam was Jake's father. Neil had been devastated when their vet had told him that Sam had a heart problem. Normally, Sam, not Jake, would have made the journey with them to Blackpool to see their old friends Max Hooper and Prince, but they'd decided it was just too risky. The excitement might have been too much for poor old Sam.

"I've got butterflies in my stomach," said Emily.

"About leaving Sam?" asked Neil.

"No. About staying at Max's house. Do you think it'll be really fancy?" Now it was Emily's turn to sound worried. Jake whimpered in her arms while he dozed, as if in sympathy.

Neil and Emily had met Max Hooper and his

golden cocker spaniel, Prince, when the actor and his dog had come to Compton to make an episode of the popular TV series *The Time Travelers*. They all had become good friends, and Neil and Emily had been thrilled to get an invitation to Max's house near Blackpool.

"I thought Max's mom and dad were great when we met them at the show's screening," said Neil. "They're really nice. And even though Max does all that TV stuff, *he's* not stuck up at all!"

The train was slowing down as it passed through the suburbs of Blackpool on its way to the station. On a huge billboard by the side of the track, a massive poster shouted *SUPERDOG!* in tall black letters.

"Hey, there's a poster for the show," Neil yelled. Jake woke up, stretched, and put his paws up to the window so that he could look, too.

"Wow," said Emily, "you certainly couldn't miss that, could you? It's enough to make anyone want to go there right now."

On the billboard was a painting of an energetic, superfit Border collie bounding onto a seesaw with a smiling owner running along at its side. SUPERDOG! THE BLACKPOOL FAIRGROUNDS. JULY 29TH–31ST. BE THERE! the poster demanded.

With a squeal of its brakes, the train came to a halt, and a muffled voice muttered something through the echoing station speakers.

"What was that he said?" asked Emily.

"Remember to take your luggage with you! It's what they always say," Neil replied.

"Have we got everything?" asked Emily, grabbing her jacket and shoulder bag.

"I think so," said Neil.

"I'll look after Jake," said Emily.

"And I'll carry Jake's suitcase," said Neil. That morning, he had packed a case with everything Jake might need for four days away — his blanket, his bowl, his two favorite toys, his usual canned food, and assorted healthy treats. The list seemed to go on and on.

"It's easy to tell which case is Jake's," said Neil, struggling onto the platform with a bag in each hand. "It's the heavy one."

"Hey, there they are!" cried Emily, pointing down the platform.

Max Hooper and Prince were waiting at the end of the platform by the ticket booth. Max was looking as cool as ever, in a designer sweatshirt, jeans, and sneakers. Max's parents were there, too. Alex Hooper, tall, balding, and in his early forties, peered down the platform searching for them. He stood head and shoulders above his petite and friendly-looking wife, Sue, who smiled and waved as Emily and Neil caught sight of them approaching.

"Welcome to sunny Blackpool!" said Max, greeting Neil and Emily with friendly hugs and handshakes.

Prince bounced around on the end of his leash, excited. "Jake's grown a lot since I saw him last!"

"He's getting bigger every day, believe me," said Neil.

Jake barked a friendly greeting, too.

Max was struggling to hold back his energetic cocker spaniel. Prince's front paws skidded around on the smooth tarmac in his eagerness to smother all his old friends with slobbery affection. "Hey, easy, Prince! Give Jake a few minutes to get used to you!"

Neil put his bags down. "You're only being friendly, aren't you?" he said softly, bending to stroke Prince's beautiful golden ears. "Here, Jake, come and say hello to my favorite cocker spaniel!"

Prince loomed over Jake and sniffed him inquisitively. Jake drew back toward Emily for a second but

then shyly moved forward again, his tail wagging furiously.

"Watch your backs," commanded a gruff voice. A tall fellow strode right through the middle of the little gathering of people, headed in the direction of the parking lot. From where Neil was crouched, he could see only an absolutely massive pair of dirty boots, which missed one of Jake's paws by a hair's width. Jake leaped away, squealing in surprise.

In an instant, Prince turned and bared his teeth in an angry growl. Just for a moment, Neil was afraid that the newcomer might aim a kick at Prince or that Prince might bite a convenient leg, but Max was on the alert and pulled the dog to his side.

The young man turned around and wagged a finger. "You need to keep your animal under control," he scolded as he walked away.

"Hmm," said Alex Hooper. "Sorry, Neil and Emily. We're not all like that here."

"Those posters for Superdog! are everywhere, aren't they?" said Neil as the Hoopers' car purred smoothly out of town.

"Yeah. It's making me feel nervous," said Max.

"You? Nervous?" said Emily incredulously. "I'd have thought you'd be used to it all by now."

"Well, I'm used to being on the set when we're making *The Time Travelers*," said Max, "but this is different. Doing live public appearances is a real chore. And this weekend they want Prince and me to do all kinds of stuff for some new program they've dreamed up. Interviews. Links. We won't know exactly what we'll have to do till we meet the producer at the fairgrounds tomorrow."

"It's quite a challenge, isn't it, Max?" said his mom. "But you *are* excited, aren't you?"

"Yes. Just very nervous."

"Well, I'm certainly looking forward to watching three whole days of dog competitions," said Neil enthusiastically.

"It all looks very exciting," agreed Emily.

Prince licked Max's face and then tried to climb over the seats toward Jake. Jake shrank back into Neil's elbow and whined.

"Come on, Jake." Neil laughed. "He's not going to hurt you!" Jake poked his head out again, as if playing hide-and-seek. "Tell me again, Max," Neil went on. "I didn't quite get it on the phone. Why is Superdog! so different from any of the other dog shows I might have seen before?"

"Sounds like *you* should be doing the interviewing," said Max. "You're the professional when it comes to dogs, Neil. You tell me! But I think they've called it Superdog! because it'll sound good on television and because someone dreamed up this idea for a big new agility event. It's spread over three days, in between the other normal parts of the show."

"So it's like the three-day events they have for

horses?" asked Emily. "With lots of different chal-
lenges?"

"Do you think the dogs like it?" said Max's dad
doubtfully.

"If they're trained by someone who knows what
they're doing, they'll love it," Neil answered.

"Sam's great," said Emily. "You should see him. I
bet if we had entered him in Superdog! he'd have
won it, no trouble. Border collies always do well."

"He *used* to be great," Neil said quietly and sadly,
stroking Jake. Being at an agility competition without Sam was a painful reminder for Neil of just how
sick Jake's dad really was.

Max's family lived in a big old house, surrounded by
tall shady poplars on the edge of a village.

"I told you they'd be fancy," Emily confided to Neil
just before dinner. "My room's got its own bathroom.
What's yours like?"

"Well, I'm in with Max," Neil answered. "His
room's really excellent. He's got his own computer!"

"Do you think Jake'll be all right tonight?" said
Emily, bending down to pet the puppy. "He's never
been away from home before, and the house must
seem kind of big and scary."

"He'll be fine. Won't you, Jake?" said Neil. Jake put
his head to one side and then tried to chase his tail
madly until he fell over. "Always the comedian!" Neil
laughed.

"Do you want to go down to the South Pier tonight?" Max asked over dinner. "Dad's eager to take us into Blackpool, and there's a great amusement park there. If the weather stays nice, it'll be a really good time."

"Yes, please!" said Neil and Emily together.

"Why don't you leave Jake with us?" said Max's mom. "Prince is used to crashes and bangs from being on set, but I'm not sure Jake'll enjoy the fun of the rides. He'll be much better off staying here. On second thought, maybe Prince should stay, too. They seem to be getting along really well."

As if in agreement, Jake woofed loudly and chased Prince's tail a few times before turning to face him, looking for a game. Prince put his head to one side and studied Jake thoughtfully. Then he shook himself and walked away from the younger dog as if to say, *I dunno. These puppies!*

It was a wonderful warm and starry summer evening. They all agreed that eating an ice-cream cone on a night like this, surrounded by the sparkling lights of Blackpool, was an excellent way to spend their time. The amusement park was crowded, everyone seemed happy, and the three friends made themselves dizzy on the rides.

"Let's find somewhere a little quieter," said Max eventually. "I don't know about you, but I'm going deaf." They never seemed to be out of earshot of loud music wherever they went.

"What's happening over there?" Neil had noticed a crowd of people around a stand near the edge of the park.

"Search me," said Max. "Let's go and take a look."

On a raised platform, they saw the equipment for a miniature adventure playground. The whole stand was lit as brightly as if it was a stage.

"It's a jungle gym," explained Emily. "They had one at the May Fair in Compton. But why's everyone watching?"

They didn't have to wait long for an answer. An elegant, beautifully groomed, black-and-tan-colored mongrel bounded onto the platform, followed by a tall slim girl of about eleven, dressed in pink dungarees. She bowed to the audience as music swelled from speakers to the left and right of the platform. Then her dog began to swoop up and down and over the jungle gym at the girl's every command. It was spellbinding. The dog never once took a wrong step. It seemed to defy gravity, balancing when the girl told it to, in places Neil thought would be impossible, and jumping fearlessly over any obstacle in its way. Dog and human seemed to understand each other perfectly.

"It's . . . it's like a ballet," said Emily.

Neil snorted. "It's much better than that. They're

*unbelievable*. Have you ever seen anything like it before, Max?"

Max had to agree that he hadn't. And obviously neither had the rest of the crowd. When the girl and her canine partner had finished and come back to the front of the stage to bow, everyone whooped and whistled and hollered. Money clattered into the bucket the girl was holding. The girl laughed out loud and threw the dog a treat. As they left the stage, Neil could have sworn the dog was smiling, too.

"Hang on a minute," he said to the other two, "I've just got to tell her how fantastic that was."

"I think he must be in love." Max laughed.

"Ugh," said Emily. Then she added, "Only with the dog. You'll see!"

"Hello," said Neil, rushing up to the girl and her dog as they paused beside the stage. "That was amazing. What's his name?"

"Twister," she said. "And I'm Becky. Becky Aslett. And thank you. We love being watched, don't we, Twister? *And* we like compliments."

Twister barked, as if in agreement, and nuzzled up to Neil. Neil took Twister's face in his hands and scratched him under the chin. The big dog's eyes were sparkling brightly. He was marvelous.

"How long have you been training him?" asked Neil, stroking the muscular dog's big pointed ears.

"Two years. But he only competed in Agility for the first time this year."

"He looks very strong. And fast. How old is he?"

"Nearly four years old now," answered Becky, beaming with pride.

"I don't suppose —" Neil started to ask a question but was interrupted by a sudden yell from a few yards away. A thin, pale boy stood facing them with a scowl on his face. At his side sat a German shepherd dog, its teeth bared.

"Oh, not again!" Neil thought he heard Becky say under her breath.

"Hey, you!" the boy shouted again.

Becky tried to ignore the newcomer for a moment,

then gave in and fixed him with a glare. "What do *you* want, Marty?" she said in a bored voice.

"You've got no chance tomorrow," the boy taunted. "Do you hear me? You and your mutt! Go back where you came from. Get it? If you know what's good for you!"

The boy cackled, called the German shepherd to heel, and elbowed his way off through the crowd.

Becky looked thrown for a moment by what had happened. She stared after the boy for a few seconds before turning back to Neil. "Sorry," she said. "You were just asking me something?"

"I was just going to say, I don't suppose you're here for Superdog!, are you?"

Becky looked at him in surprise and then said almost triumphantly, "Yeah. How do you know about Superdog!? That's absolutely what we're here for! You're going to be the champ, aren't you, Twister? And that's what makes poor old Marty and Buster so upset. We're going to win Superdog! and not them! You wait and see."

# CHAPTER TWO

**"I** was worried about you at the park last night," Max said to Neil at breakfast. "I thought there was going to be trouble there for a minute."

"Me, too," added Emily, yawning. "That Marty was horrible."

It was eight-thirty on Friday morning. Alex Hooper had driven off to work in Manchester hours ago, but everyone else was sitting around the Hoopers' kitchen table munching cornflakes and toast. They all looked and felt the worse for wear. All except Jake!

The whole night long — and without an ounce of success — they'd tried to settle Jake down. For the first few hours, while he'd been in his basket next to Prince in the downstairs utility room, the large house had echoed to the puppy's heart-wrenching howls. Several times during the long night, Neil had pulled the blankets over his ears and tried to tell himself Jake would soon stop complaining and go to sleep. But who could leave a puppy alone and sad like that? So, every now and then, he'd tiptoed down to cuddle Jake, trying to persuade him that he was safe in this big, new house with its creaking noises and interesting smells.

But each time, as soon as Neil had crept back into bed, the eerie sound would start again. Eventually, Sue Hooper had relented, and Jake had been allowed into Max and Neil's room, though as their yawns showed now, Plan B hadn't worked very well, either.

This morning, Jake was in better shape than any of the humans. Mischievously bright-eyed and bushy-tailed, he was darting and diving around Prince's legs, playing some imaginary game. Prince ignored him loftily.

"There's nothing wrong with Marty's *dog*," said Neil defensively. "Buster's fine, according to Becky. It's Marty that's got the problem. From what she's seen, he's desperate for someone to pay attention to him. Probably because no one in his family does."

"That's no excuse," Max replied. "I can't stand people with bad attitudes."

"Well, apparently, when they've met at other dog shows, Twister and Buster have been a good match for each other. And since they're both hot contenders for Superdog!," said Neil with a smile, "you might find yourself having to be nice to Marty very soon. Good luck!"

After they finished their breakfast, they climbed into the Hoopers' car with Jake and Prince for the short trip down to the fairgrounds to meet Mike Bishop, the producer of the *Superdog!* TV program.

Sue Hooper turned off the main road and they made their way through a mass of trailers and minivans to a parking lot. Next to it was an open arena marked with white painted fences. On two sides there were covered stands where spectators could watch the events without getting wet. By the entrance stood a bearded man wearing a sweater and brown corduroys. He was pacing up and down, studying his watch anxiously.

"I bet that's Mike Bishop," joked Max. "TV producers always look the same. They all wear brown corduroys and Hush Puppies. I think it's a sort of uniform."

They climbed out of the car.

"I'll park, then I'll be over at your aunt's refreshment stand if you need me, Max," said Sue Hooper. "I promised her I'd help set up."

She sped away in a spectacular cloud of dust, and Max called Neil and Emily over to introduce them to Mike Bishop.

"Can you two amuse yourselves for a while — ?"

began Max after they'd shaken hands, but he was quickly interrupted by Jake nuzzling his knee. "Sorry, Jake, I didn't mean to forget you." Max laughed. "Can you *three* find something to do while Mike tells Prince and me what he wants us to do?"

"No problem," Neil answered. "Becky's probably around somewhere. She said she'd watch for us. We'll see if we can find her. Won't we, Jake?"

Jake jumped up, wagging his tail enthusiastically.

"*I* see . . ." said Max, smiling. "Off to see Becky?"

"Oh, stop," Neil said, reddening slightly. "It's Twister I'm interested in."

"What did I tell you yesterday?" Emily said, laughing at Max.

Around the edge of the arena, people were pulling tents into position, trying not to get run over by the truck delivering crates of food and soda.

Neil and Emily watched a striking-looking woman with a matching floral skirt and headscarf bullying a male companion into putting up a sign outside one of the tents. The sign read: MYSTIC MIRYAM VAVASOUR AND GYPSY ROSE: PET PSYCHICS. WE SEE THE FUTURE. OTHERS ONLY DREAM.

"Up a little," she shouted at him, hands on her hips. "Down a little. Move your hand. No, it's still not straight. Maybe you should come down here, hon, and let me do it."

The man muttered under his breath.

"What on earth is a pet psychic?" asked Emily as they approached.

"Someone who can tell your pet's fortune, I suppose," said Neil. "What a joke!"

A Jack Russell terrier with a black patch over one eye scurried out of the tent and approached Jake, nose twitching, tail and bottom wagging like crazy. The Jack Russell came as close as it could to Jake's face and then lay down with outstretched paws, staring hypnotically at the puppy from its one good eye. Until then, Jake had been practically pulling Neil off his feet from the end of the leash, but now, fixed by the terrier's gaze, he recoiled for an instant. Then, to Neil's surprise, Jake relaxed and squatted amiably head-to-head with the stranger. Suddenly, it was as if the two were old friends.

"Well, you're a character, aren't you, old girl? I wonder what's wrong with that eye of yours?" said Neil softly, reaching down to ruffle the terrier's neck.

The newcomer ignored him completely, holding Jake's attention with her steady gaze.

"Rose! What are you up to, Rose?" It was the woman in the flowered skirt. "Rose is all right," she went on, calling over to Neil and Emily as she came toward them. "She doesn't mean anything by it. My, that's a lovely puppy you've got there. What's his name?"

"Jake!" said Neil. "His name's Jake."

Neil looked at the sign again. A picture of an adorably cute Jack Russell with an eye patch was painted on it. "And your dog . . . ?"

The woman's gaze followed Neil's. ". . . is called Gypsy Rose. That's right, dear."

"And is she really psychic?" Emily asked.

The woman smiled. "Well, when we're open later on, you'll have to come and find out, won't you, my dear? And make sure you bring Jake with you. Now then, Rose, stop bothering these nice people."

Gypsy Rose pulled herself up, stretched, and trotted off with her owner. Jake never moved an inch.

"That's better. That's what I call straight," the woman shouted to the man up the ladder. "But why did it take you all day?"

Neil, Emily, and Jake stared at her as if they were in a trance. Only Becky's shout of welcome dragged them back to reality.

"I see you've met Miryam," she said as Twister bounced and twirled around her.

Neil got down on his knees and gave the energetic dog a warm hello, scratching his tummy until the dog rolled over submissively. "I think he likes me!"

"I think he does," said Becky. "My mom's got some snacks over in our trailer. Want to come?" And with Twister leading the way, they picked their way through the maze of the fairgrounds campsite.

It was a tight squeeze for the four of them and the two dogs inside Becky and her mom's trailer. If it had been wider, it would have been cozy. In midsummer, it was definitely too warm for comfort, even with the windows and both doors open. The walls of the trailer were festooned with quilts embroidered with explosions of warm colors: reds, purples, and violets. Angela Aslett watched Emily's mouth drop open and laughed. "Do you like them?" she asked.

"They're wonderful," Emily exclaimed. "Where did you get them?"

"Mom made them," Becky said proudly. "She's an artist. She sells them for lots of money."

Angela shook her head. "Oh, Becky. Don't exaggerate!" She ruffled her daughter's hair affectionately as she spoke. Twister growled softly and sniffed Jake, who cowered back under Neil's knees.

Neil put a hand down to comfort the puppy and said, "It must be amazing to live in a trailer. Is it your home all the time?"

"Yes," Becky replied. "Although we're usually in Kent on my uncle's land. That's where I go to school."

"And you move around the country going to fairs and shows? That's so cool," said Emily.

"The jungle gym helps pay our way a little, too," added Angela. "It's very popular and gas is expensive, you know!"

Neil and Emily laughed.

"So do you meet Buster and Marty a lot, then?" asked Neil.

"We see them around," said Becky, rolling her eyes. "They have a house in Kent as well and drive around in a big, ugly trailer. You'll know it when you see it — it's huge!"

Twister got up and shook his head vigorously. Neil suspected he wanted to play some more!

"Twister doesn't seem quite so sure." Emily laughed.

Neil had slipped the leash off Jake while they'd been talking, and the puppy had been nestling comfortably between his knees. But now, disturbed by Twister's large body moving close to him in the confined space, Jake somehow wriggled free. To Neil's astonishment, before he could lay a hand on him, Jake was out of the trailer door and tearing away across the parking lot. Neil shouted desperately after him, "Jake! Stay!" but Jake paused for only a few seconds, looked around, and then scampered off again.

It was a moment before anyone moved. There was no point in going after him. Jake might be only eight months old, but none of them could run as fast as a determined Border collie among all the trailers and stands. Becky was quick to take in Neil's helpless expression and was soon on her feet.

"Twister! Go! Find!" she said, pushing Twister out of the door and away across the grass. "Don't worry," she said to Neil. "He's got Jake's scent. He'll bring him back safely. You'll see."

"I really don't know what's gotten into Jake," Neil muttered, his stomach a tight knot of anxiety. "He's normally so reliable." He watched Twister run fast and purposefully along the grass walkways and plunge into a throng of people, near where Jake had disappeared.

"He's still only a puppy," said Becky's mom soothingly. "And I don't expect he's been away from home much, has he? You've got to make allowances. It must be very strange for him."

"Maybe," Neil grumbled. "But he should still know better."

In front of them, though the campsite was full of activity, there was no sign of either dog. They waited anxiously by the trailer steps. Neil shifted from foot to foot miserably, thinking of the awful things that could happen to Jake in the fairground traffic. Then, at last, from the distance came a single reassuring bark.

"That's Twister," Becky cried. "He must have caught up with Jake."

There was another agonizingly long wait. The horn of a truck blared, and Emily clutched Neil's arm. Then, from behind a fence twenty yards away, Twister appeared, ears pricked, and sprang over to them, panting loudly.

"Good boy," said Becky, producing a treat from her pocket and slipping it into Twister's mouth. The dog crunched it quickly.

"But where's Jake?" said Neil, fidgeting nervously.

A few seconds later, looking as if he hadn't a care in the world, Jake finally sauntered around the corner on Twister's trail. He nuzzled up to the older dog, then to Neil.

"Twister, you're a genius," Neil trumpeted. "And you," he scolded Jake, "you should say you're sorry for the trouble you've caused. What on earth did you think you were doing?"

Jake looked suitably ashamed of himself and quickly settled down in a corner beside Twister's basket.

After some chocolate cake, Neil and Emily thanked Becky's mom and went to find Max and Prince, promising to catch up with Becky before the first round of Superdog! started later that afternoon.

"Don't miss it!" said Becky. "We need all the support we can get."

"We'll be there, don't you worry," promised Neil. "It'll be great to have someone to cheer for."

A small crowd of people was gathered around the

Northwest Television van outside the arena entrance.

"I don't believe it," said Neil, when they were near enough to see what was going on. "Would you look at that?"

Staring aggressively at Mike Bishop was Marty. His German shepherd dog sat alertly at his side, and beside them stood another boy. He looked just like Marty, only much taller, several pounds heavier, and a whole lot nastier. Mike Bishop seemed to be unaware of their presence.

Neil strolled over to Max. "What's happening? You

know that's the fellow who was such a pain at the station yesterday, don't you?"

"Well, it's Marty's brother, Gary, apparently," said Max. As he spoke, the older boy strode forward and began talking menacingly to Mike Bishop.

The producer took a step backward, and they heard him say, "*We* make the decisions about who we talk to, thank you very much. If your dog does well, maybe we *will* want a feature on him. Maybe he *will* end up being a TV star. But we make up our own minds. Am I making myself clear?"

"It isn't *if* he wins, pal, it's *when*," shouted Marty's brother. "Isn't that right, Marty?"

Marty looked as if he wasn't too sure he wanted to be there. He shifted around away from his brother and shrugged a sort of "yes." Marty's brother turned around to anyone who wanted to listen and hollered, "Remember where you heard it first. Whatever this guy says, there's only one winner here this weekend, and you're looking at him. It's Buster! The rest of them might as well go home. Come on, Marty, let's split." And he pushed through the crowd, with Marty and Buster following him uncertainly.

"I never knew these competitions were taken so seriously," said Max with a frown.

"Oh, yes, a lot of people take these competitions *very* seriously," said Neil ominously. "And they'll do anything to win."

# CHAPTER THREE

**N**eil and Emily ate their bag lunches in the shade of a large tree behind the TV equipment vans. The fairgrounds had been hot and dusty, and it was a treat to hide out away from the hustle and bustle of the growing numbers of entrants and spectators.

By one-thirty, they were all raring to go again, Prince and Jake included. Prince looked every inch a TV dog, his coat shining like gold in the sunlight. Neil admired the intelligence and alertness in his eyes. The dog seemed to know the cameras would be on him very soon. Max said good-bye and went off to start work.

The arena was almost ready for action, and people and animals were streaming through the gate to compete or watch from the stands.

Neil spotted Becky nearby, leaning on a rail and studying the course. Dressed in Lycra and with her running shoes hanging around her neck, she looked like the perfect athlete.

"Where's Twister?" Neil asked anxiously. "There's nothing wrong with him, is there?"

"Yeah," said Becky. "He decided he couldn't face his fans."

Just for a split second, Neil wasn't sure if she was joking.

"Lighten up, Neil." Becky laughed. "This is Twister we're talking about, not Jake. Actually, he's back at the trailer getting prettied up by Mom. We're drawn to run first, so I'm just making sure I've got the course down in my head. We walked it half an hour ago, but I hate leaving anything to chance."

"What do you think of the course?" asked Emily.

"I've seen easier," said Becky, narrowing her eyes against the sunlight. "But then, this is supposed to be a top competition."

In front of them was an assortment of jumps. Some were obviously designed to test how high the dogs could leap, and some to see how good they were at long jumping. In among the jumps were a couple of tunnels. One had a kink in it, and one ended in what looked like a sack. Then there were two sets of weaving poles where the dogs had to slalom in and out like a skier.

"So today is just jumping?" asked Neil.

"Yes. The other stuff comes tomorrow and Sunday," Becky replied. "But remember, it's not just getting over the jumps any old way. It's getting over them, not knocking any poles down, *and* doing it all in under ninety seconds. And *that's* hard, believe me."

Neil nodded. He knew all about the excitement and pressure of running beside your partner against the clock, getting the order of the obstacles right, and having to issue precise commands.

Suddenly, they were all aware of Marty and Buster walking past. Becky turned to them and called, "Hi, Marty! Good luck later on!"

Marty blushed slightly, dropped his eyes, and grunted, all without breaking step.

"He really can't help it, you know," Becky said when he'd gone. "The whole family is odd, particularly his older brother. They all seem to turn up for competitions and shows regularly, but nobody's got a clue how they make a living. I wonder whether they've told Marty that Buster's got to earn his keep. There's a thousand-dollar prize for the winner of Superdog! and the chance of some paid advertising work afterward."

"Wow," said Neil. "That's serious money."

Becky laughed. "I wouldn't exactly say no to it, either! I'm really more interested in the competing than the money, though." She looked at her watch. "Time for action," she said. "I've got to go and get

Twister. We're on in ten minutes. I'll expect to hear you all shouting and cheering Twister on."

There were a few hundred spectators dotted around the arena now, and as Neil, Emily, and Jake found a good vantage point near the front, the loudspeakers banged and crackled to life. The TV cameras swung around onto the master of ceremonies, who announced grandly that Max Hooper and his dog, Prince, stars of television's *Time Travelers*, would open the show by lighting the competition flame.

In the corner of the arena, between the stands, a large metal bowl had been set on a platform. Neil and Emily watched as Max, with Prince at his side, walked slowly to the bowl holding a lit candle high in his right hand. As he touched the bowl, a spurt of flame shot upward, and the crowd applauded. At the side of the bowl, an electronic scoreboard lit up, flashing the message WELCOME TO SUPERDOG!, and an animation of a Border collie bounced across the screen.

Then officials dressed in blazers and white trousers ran around on the course, and they heard the emcee say, "Now let's give a big hand to competitor number one for the opening round of this weekend's major competition: Superdog! And here they are . . . Twister with his partner, eleven-year-old Becky Aslett . . ."

The cameras from Northwest Television pointed at Becky and Twister as they prepared to run.

"Don't they look great?" Neil whispered.

"Which one, Becky or Twister?" said Emily with a smile.

"Cut it out," Neil said, becoming a little tired of his sister's teasing. "*Both* of them!"

Becky and Twister positioned themselves at the starting line, and the arena went pin-drop quiet. Then a bell sounded and Twister was off, moving quickly into his stride.

The first two jumps were easy — really only warm-ups for what was to come — and Twister sailed over them. There was nothing fussy or extravagant in his movement. He simply flowed. The course zigged and zagged, and with Becky just ahead of him, every turn Twister made was as tight as it could be. He flashed through the first set of six weaving poles and dived into the first tunnel with such style that the crowd roared its appreciation. Everything was going brilliantly. Then, out of nowhere, came a problem.

Becky was back-pedaling, drawing Twister around to the next series of higher, more difficult jumps, when her foot caught on a tuft of grass, and she stumbled and lost her balance. For a moment, Neil could see Twister was confused, as Becky let her concentration falter in her determination not to fall over. The whole crowd drew in their breath. But like a true gymnast, she put one hand on the ground to steady herself, drawing Twister onto the next fence.

Neil found that his fists were clenched with tension as the pair fought the huge clock that ticked away remorselessly at the side of the course. It showed just thirty seconds remaining.

"They *have* to do it in time," Neil muttered. "Come on, Becky! Go, Twister!" Jake added his encouragement with a loud bark.

There were only five seconds left as they came to the final fence.

"They can make it! Go for it, Twister!" shouted Neil. There was a rising swell of noise from the

crowd as Twister leaped at the last and longest jump. He flew through the air, but in a heart-stopping moment his trailing leg caught the bar and brought it down.

The crowd gasped.

As Becky and Twister crossed the finish line, the clock on the scoreboard stopped at eighty-nine seconds. They'd completed the round with just five faults against them for the one bar down.

"Will it be good enough?" asked Emily.

"Who knows?" said Neil. "But Becky looks pretty happy, doesn't she?"

They could see Becky making a huge fuss over Twister in the competitors' circle. She caught sight of Neil and Emily and waved, signaling that they should come down and meet her outside the arena.

When they found them, Becky was teasing Twister, tumbling around with him on a clear patch of grass as her mom looked on indulgently.

"Well done! You were really excellent!" Neil said enthusiastically. "But what did *you* think?"

"Good," said Becky, dusting herself off as Jake took over playing with Twister. "Very good. It's going to be hard for everybody out there. Some of the jumps toward the end are asking a lot of the dogs. They're *so* high. And the longer the dogs are kept waiting to run, the harder it'll be. There really isn't enough shade in that enclosure."

"Yes, I noticed that," said Neil. "You'd think they

would get that right at an event like this, wouldn't you?" He changed the subject, anxious not to lose Twister and Becky to other admirers who were gathering around them. "What are you going to do now?" Neil asked.

"Well, I *don't* want to stay here and watch the other dogs. It makes me more nervous than running the course." Becky laughed. "Anyway, the better competitors are scheduled near the end. Let's take Twister for a short walk. We don't want him stiffening up."

Twister whined his agreement, rolled over, and stood up.

Becky's mom said she'd stay behind to keep an eye on the opposition, and the rest of them strolled out to the ice-cream stalls and burger stands.

For many people, the show seemed to be an excuse for a general day out. There were more people wandering around outside than sitting inside the arena. After saying hello to Mrs. Hooper at her sister's refreshment stall, they eventually found themselves next to Miryam the Pet Psychic's tent.

"Let's go in," pleaded Emily. "Miryam said to be sure to bring Jake to see her."

Neil looked doubtful.

"Go on!" said Becky. "Don't be a spoilsport! It'll be fun. She keeps turning up at these shows, and I've always wanted to see what she's up to in that tent of hers!"

Their minds were made up for them as Miryam

wobbled into the sunshine. "You've come to see me, my dears. Me and my Gypsy Rose," she boomed. "How nice, how lovely!" She squinted at the three children and two dogs. "It'll be a tight squeeze. And the vibrations may be a bit confusing, but I expect we'll manage. Now, who's first?"

Inside the tent it was creepily dark. The sides and ceiling were draped in heavy maroon curtains. Sticks of incense burned in each corner, filling the tent with a dense and heady perfume. Miryam sat down behind a table on which stood a ball of misty, frosted glass. Neil wanted to reach out and touch it, but he didn't dare. Next to Miryam, on her own chair, sat Gypsy Rose, complete with eye patch.

The friends sat shoulder to shoulder. Miryam had obviously taken a real liking to Jake, and she almost snatched him out of Neil's arms. Jake whimpered for a second, holding himself rigid, but then, as she stroked his neck, he relaxed. Miryam closed her eyes and passed her hands over Jake's body, once, twice, three times. Then, as if she was warming herself, she placed her hands on either side of the glass ball. From somewhere deep in Gypsy Rose's throat there came a long, slow, warm rumble, like a murmur of approval.

"What a strong aura you have, young Jake. What force!"

Neil smiled. *This is what they all say,* he thought. Miryam's voice sounded distant. "And there's brightness there, too. I see your feet running fast. You will bring your family a lot of pleasure. And a little anxiety, too."

Miryam had been smiling, but then her face changed suddenly, as if a cloud had passed across the sun.

"What's the matter, Miryam? Tell us!" Neil said after a few seconds. He tensed slightly.

"There are some shadows here. Perhaps some illness close at hand to Jake?" Miryam said thoughtfully.

Neil whispered, "Sam!" His pulse started to race, his hands were shaking, and he began to wish they hadn't come to see Miryam after all.

Miryam frowned. "The image is fading. There are too many shadows." Her face was creasing into an intense stare. "I can't reach it." She peered into the glass ball, as if trying to see something a long way off.

Then Miryam relaxed and sat back in her chair. She looked at Neil, her face soft with sympathy. Neil fought back the tears.

"What will be, will be," she said quietly. "There is a time for all of us." She laid her hand on Neil's across the table.

Becky looked on, puzzled, not knowing quite what to say or do. After all, she had never met Sam, had never even heard of him, and so hadn't the slightest idea what might be wrong. After a moment's pause, she asked brightly, "Will you do Twister now? Tell us what you see in *his* future!"

Neil made a huge effort to pull himself together. "Yes," he said bravely. "Is Twister going to be Superdog? Tell us about all the prizes he's going to win! We've got to know." And he forced his face into a smile.

When Becky began to ask Miryam about Twister, a low, throaty growl came once more from Gypsy Rose. This time the sound was raspy and threatening, not warm and soothing at all. Miryam was silent and still, taking her time, apparently thinking about what to say, until Twister broke the spell. He shifted on his bottom and began to pant loudly.

Miryam looked up sharply at Neil and Becky, her eyes dark and penetrating. By now the smile had faded from Becky's face. Neil shivered. Surely there couldn't be more bad news?

Miryam spoke briskly, but not unkindly. "I told you the vibrations might be confusing. I can't tell you any more. You'll have to come back another time." And she dropped her eyes, avoiding Becky's gaze.

Becky wouldn't let it go. "I don't believe you," she said. "You've seen something else, haven't you? You've got to tell us. You can't let us not know."

Miryam paused, head bowed for a moment. Then she looked at Becky again and spoke slowly and thoughtfully. "It's not a science, my dear. What I do is more like painting a picture, you know. Sometimes the outlines of what I paint are as clear as real life. Sometimes all I can feel is a blur of colors."

"And Twister?"

"All I see is that the colors are mixed up. And though your Twister may become a great champion, it won't be without a struggle. There may be difficult times ahead for you both."

Becky looked crestfallen.

Miryam threw her arms into the air. "You see. You didn't want to know, did you? This is what is so hard for me. People don't like hearing bad news." She sounded exasperated. Then she softened. "But please, remember one thing." She waited until she was sure she held everyone's attention. "We *can* change the future, all of us. If we're smart and we really want to!"

## CHAPTER FOUR

**O**utside the pet psychic's tent, the sunlight was blinding. Unsure about how to interpret what they had just heard, Neil, Emily, and Becky stumbled around the fairgrounds in a daze for half an hour, looking at the various stalls until finally they decided to find Becky's mom.

When Angela saw them at the arena, she thought the friends must have fallen out with one another, they seemed so glum. "Everything OK?" she asked anxiously.

"Yeah, fine." Becky sounded casual, even if her face didn't match her words. "What's the news?"

Her mom looked at her sideways, surprised to hear Becky sounding so down. "Well, you've arrived just in time," she said. "Two more to run, and

Buster's the first of the two. But you're still in front, aren't you, Twister? Clever old thing!" She bent and patted Twister, who barked his approval loudly.

"Excellent!" said Neil. "I knew they'd find you hard to beat."

Pulling herself together as best she could, Becky covered her eyes in pretend panic. "I can't bear to watch!" she said.

Neil looked critically at Buster and Marty as they entered the ring. There was something about the way Buster carried himself that told you he was a strong and willing animal. *He's an honest trier,* thought Neil. *You know he'd always give you a hundred percent.* And it was obvious that, for all of his faults, Marty had Buster's total trust and devotion. Yet somehow there was still something lacking. Perhaps Buster just wasn't smart enough? Or was the problem Marty? He certainly wasn't in great shape, observed Neil. He wasn't what you'd call a natural athlete!

Marty and Buster were doing well over the first half of the course, though — well enough for Becky to look worried. But as Marty wheezed and puffed his way into the second minute, Buster's turns became sloppy and wide, and Marty's commands less decisive. Then, at the third jump from the end, Marty made Buster turn in too tightly, and he crashed through the poles with a clatter. The crowd "oohed" and "aahed" in disappointment. Becky gave a little leap in the air and gasped, "Yes!" quietly to herself. Somehow Buster held himself together to make the last two jumps safely, but now there were time faults to be added as well.

"They've all been having trouble getting inside ninety seconds," said Becky's mom. "I think only one dog other than Twister hasn't had a time penalty, and she hit tons of obstacles!"

To polite applause, the event announcer told the crowd that Buster's run put him second behind Twister and Becky Aslett. The electronic scoreboard flashed Twister's name in large letters ahead of the names of the trailing competitors. But how long would it stay there? More clapping heralded the arrival in the arena of the last competitor to run — a Mr. Barry Carpenter and his dog, Shannon.

Becky snorted. "What a name! Shannon! Sounds more like a pop singer than a dog."

*Barry Carpenter isn't up to much, either,* thought Neil. He was small and balding and dressed in country clothes. But from the starting bell, Neil could see that this pair were real contenders. Shannon was a Border collie, and, from the look of her owner, she might have been a farm dog. She was fit, muscular, and lean, with all the intelligence and skill that Neil loved in the breed. Shannon scarcely seemed to move as she covered the jumps with grace and great speed. Her partner's commands were issued so quietly you could hardly hear them, but there was no doubting the understanding between the two. Now Becky really looked anxious, and with good reason.

Relief followed when Shannon went too hard at the second and longer set of weaving poles and failed to make it through one of the gates properly. You could see the frustration on Barry Carpenter's face. Perfection — *winning* — really mattered to him. Taking part wasn't enough.

As the pair came to a jump near the finish line, something strange happened. They were cruising, well inside the ninety seconds, and Shannon seemed to be handling things well. She soared up, apparently clearing the jump easily, and, yet, as she glided onto the final fence and the line, the bar dislodged and fell to the ground. Barry Carpenter shot the referee a look of appeal as Shannon finished, then marched over to him, waving his arms in anger.

Neil and Becky held their breath. They heard Barry Carpenter shouting, "But her legs were miles clear of the bar. . . ." and they could see the referee shaking his head. Then, to jeers and booing from the crowd, the result flashed up on the electronic scoreboard. At the end of the first round, despite the appeal, Shannon was in second place behind Twister.

A very red-faced Barry Carpenter, with Shannon at his side, stomped away out of the arena, muttering angrily. Neil, Becky, Emily, and her mom all breathed again. Twister and Jake barked a fanfare of pleasure.

"I don't think Shannon touched it," Neil said honestly.

Becky stuck out her chin. "So what!" she said. "That's what competition's all about. Taking the rough with the smooth."

"I hope," said her mom solemnly, "that I don't have to remind you of that some day, Rebecca!"

Then, thinking back to their time with Miryam, Neil boasted to Emily, "You see. All that psychic stuff's a lot of garbage, just like I told you. Twister's got it in the bag!"

That evening, there was a reception in one of the tents for everyone taking part in Superdog! Northwest Television kept the cameras rolling while they all gobbled up finger rolls and "things-on-sticks." Max and Prince were wandering around with Mike Bishop, talking to anyone they thought might have something interesting to say, including Becky and Twister. Neil and Emily hovered in the background, out of camera range, making faces at Max. Max pretended not to see them.

But apart from that, most of the people at the party were adults who were talking loudly. Even the dogs seemed restless. Neil and Emily were quickly bored, and all the more because it had started to rain, trapping them with Jake in the tent.

Eventually, as it started to grow dark, the rain

stopped and Neil, Emily, and Jake escaped into the refreshing evening air.

"I've got an idea," said Neil. "I bet they'll have left the agility course up in the arena. Let's go and find out how Jake takes to the jumps."

Emily looked doubtful. "Do you think anyone will mind?" she said.

Neil glanced back at the tent behind them. Everyone was still chatting away noisily. Some of them had even started to dance embarrassingly badly, including Mrs. Hooper and Becky's mom.

"I don't think anyone will even notice," he answered.

There was just about enough light around the arena to see where they were going. They found the lowest of the jumps and stood beside it with Jake. It seemed very high and intimidating for the puppy, even so.

"Keep Jake here," said Neil, "and I'll go around on the other side." He produced one of Jake's toys from his pocket, a very ragged bunny. Neil waved it at Jake from the far side of the jump.

"Now let him go," he said to Emily.

Jake scampered away from her, neatly side-stepped the obstacle, and rushed enthusiastically to Neil and his toy.

Neil scratched him under the ears and giggled. "No, not quite the idea, Jake. Let's try that again, shall we?"

After four or five attempts, and despite Neil show-

ing Jake how it should be done, they hadn't made much progress.

"It's still just a little too high for him, isn't it?" said Neil. "Let's try the weaving poles. He might be able to manage them."

They had great fun swerving in and out of the poles with Jake and had begun to enjoy themselves so much they didn't notice the arrival of a familiar figure.

"Hey, you," said Marty's brother, Gary. They looked up, surprised. "You shouldn't be here, you know. So clear out, understand? Competitors only."

They weren't about to argue, even though Neil was fairly sure Gary had no right to tell anyone to leave. Neil clipped Jake back onto his leash, and they made their way back to the tent as Marty's brother skulked off into the darkness.

Things were still in full swing back at the party. They found Becky sitting by the entrance to the tent with her knees drawn up, almost nodding off.

"Where's Twister?" said Neil.

"I took him back to the trailer almost an hour ago," said Becky. "I needed a break from looking after him, but it's *so* boring here. Why don't we go find a snack?"

"Will your mom mind?" asked Emily.

Becky glanced into the tent. Her mom was dancing with Barry Carpenter. His face was redder than ever. "I *think* she's enjoying herself," said Becky, grinning.

As they got near the trailer, there was less and less light to guide them. Neil was spooked by the velvety blackness. Becky took a flashlight from her jacket and shone it over the last thirty or so yards toward the door of the trailer. As the beam focused, Becky gasped in fright. The door was swinging open on its hinges, banging on the side of the trailer in the night breeze.

"Twister!" she cried out and ran ahead of Neil and Emily into the trailer.

## CHAPTER FIVE

**B**ecky scrambled up the trailer steps with Neil, Emily, and Jake on her heels. She pulled open the inner door and then sank back against the frame, her hands to her head. For a moment, Neil had no idea whether it was with relief or desperation.

"What's happened? Has Twister gone? Do we need to go and look for him?" he asked anxiously.

As he spoke, a sleepy woof came from inside and a doggy nose appeared around the door.

"Thank goodness for that," said Neil. "You had us worried for a minute there, Twister."

"I don't understand," Becky said, rubbing her forehead with one hand and stroking Twister affectionately with the other. "I know I locked the door when I came out."

"It's easy to make a mistake. I've done it before." Neil sounded offhand.

Becky looked at him sharply. "No, listen. I actually went back to check. It was locked, believe me!"

"Is anything gone from the trailer?" asked Emily.

"Dunno," said Becky, gazing around her. "Doesn't look like it. But I don't think I'd know without getting Mom to help." She clapped a hand to her mouth. "I'm going to have to tell her, aren't I? She'll go ballistic. She's always carrying on about security."

"Wouldn't Twister have been security enough, anyway?" Neil said thoughtfully. "Thieves don't generally like dogs." He inspected the outer door. "This lock doesn't look forced."

"You don't really have to force it," said Becky. "A friend used a credit card to get inside once when my mom thought she'd lost her keys. As for Twister being a guard dog, it's not what you do best, is it, Twister? And this weekend there are lots of people around who know about handling dogs." Becky stopped and looked at Twister. He'd left her and was wandering drowsily back to his basket. "I mean, I ask you, you wouldn't want *that* looking after your jewels, would you?" Twister gave a great big yawn and slumped into his blankets.

"Are you sure he's OK?" Neil asked.

"Yeah," said Becky. "He's just tired. He's always groggy after a competition."

"If you say so," said Neil. "Come on, let's go and find your mom. It'll be hard for her to be too annoyed if we're all there."

Becky looked doubtful. "You don't know my mom!" she said. "That won't stop her."

In fact, whether she was glad to escape from Barry Carpenter and his terrible dancing, or because Neil was right, Becky's mom took the news of the suspected break-in very calmly. They all traipsed through the dark back to the trailer, and Neil, Emily, and Jake waited as the Asletts checked their home.

After ten minutes, Becky's mom sank into her chair and sighed. "Well, I'm fairly sure nothing's missing."

"Perhaps they heard us coming, or saw the flashlight, and split before we got here?" said Becky.

"Maybe," Neil pondered. "It's strange, though, isn't it?" He glanced through to where Twister lay in his basket, dead to the world. It was all really very strange. He checked his watch. "Wow, Emily, it's nearly ten-thirty. We've got to go. We're supposed to be meeting Max's mom and dad up at the arena."

They said their good-byes quickly and left to find Max and his parents for their ride home.

The next morning at the Hoopers', breakfast was interrupted by the phone ringing. It was a desperate Becky asking for Neil. Calling from a pay phone on the campsite, she'd found the Hoopers' number from directory assistance. She sounded very flustered and unhappy.

"It's Twister," she blurted out. "I don't know what's the matter with him. He still seems so sleepy. He just can't be bothered with anything. We're running again at twelve, and at this rate he won't make it up to the ring!"

Neil thought hard. "Has he been sick?" he asked in a worried voice. "Are there any other very obvious symptoms? Anything you could tell a vet about?"

"Nothing very concrete." Becky sniffed. "And, anyway, there won't be a vet on-site for another couple of hours. There is one thing, though," she said slowly. "I don't know whether I'm imagining it, but his eyes look a little strange. It's like he's not focusing very well. But that's not enough to go on, is it? He's just so lethargic. Oh, Neil, what do you think I should do?"

"We'll be there just after ten," said Neil. "You've still got nearly three hours before you have to run. Why don't you take Twister for a slow, gentle walk. Try to get him warmed up a little. I don't think there's anything else you *can* do. If he's coming down with something, there won't be any help for it, Becky. You'll just have to pull out of Superdog!"

"That'd be awful," she wailed.

Becky hung up, obviously upset, and Neil went back to the breakfast table, feeling like he'd been no help at all to their new friend.

After the drive to the fairgrounds, Neil and Emily
found Becky and Twister sitting under an awning at
the side of their trailer. Neil squatted down till his
face was on a level with Twister's. "How're you doing,
old boy?" he asked. Twister halfheartedly licked
Neil's hand, then pulled away, slumping down onto
the grass.

Becky shook her head. "He's never like that. He's
always interested in people! He's just not himself,
is he?"

"You're right, Becky," said Neil. "He's not the dog
we saw yesterday afternoon."

For the next hour they walked Twister up and
down, playing with him and egging Jake on. The
younger dog pirouetted around Twister, teasing him
and even making Becky laugh. Slowly, Twister
seemed to be waking up, but as eleven-thirty approached he was still sluggish and lacking the en-
ergy he was shortly going to need so badly.

"It's now or never," said Becky. "We've got to go up
to the ring and check in. D'you think we should go
for it, anyway?" she asked her mom.

"I don't think you can do Twister any harm," her
mom replied. "If he doesn't feel up to competing, he'll
let you know soon enough. And then you'll just have to
accept the inevitable. Let's take plenty of water with
us. We mustn't let him get dehydrated in this sun."

There were already more people in the arena than
on Friday. It seemed to Neil that the atmosphere

was much more intense and intimidating than it had
been the previous day. And who should they run into
first, but Marty!

"How's your hound today?" he sneered. "Looks a
bit tired to me. I don't think he has a chance out
there, do you?" He jerked a thumb in the direction of
the rapidly filling arena.

Becky wasn't in the mood and ignored him.

*You're very talkative today, Marty,* Neil thought. *I
wonder why? And you're very quick to notice
Twister's below par.*

The arena was now laid out as the most compli-
cated test of canine agility Neil had ever seen. There
was still a set of weaving poles and some jumps, including a tire jump that looked frighteningly difficult. To these, a whole series of beautifully designed
obstacles had been added. There was an A-frame
with a peak more than two yards high; a seesaw
with a board that seemed too narrow for a dog of
Twister's large frame; a crossover table where the
competitor had to move on command to the left or
right; a couple of dog walks high off the ground, and
a pause box, where Twister would have to lie down
for ten seconds before tackling the rest of the course.

In the bright sunshine, Becky looked pale and nervous. Neil and Emily wished her and Angela Aslett
good luck, reminded Twister he was a champion in
the making, and took Jake up into the stands to wait
for Twister's turn.

This time there were ten other dogs due to run before him, including Shannon and Buster. The competitors would run in reverse order, according to their overall standing.

After all of the other entrants had completed the course with mixed success, it was Buster's turn. He was currently in third place.

From the speakers, the emcee's voice crescendoed. "And now, please welcome one of the leading contenders. Let's give a great big hand to Marty Stevens with Buster. . . ."

Emily echoed Neil's thoughts. "I'd like to give a great big boo!" she said.

But Buster was in awesome form over the obstacles. His strength and natural balance took him surefootedly over everything in his path. Marty, too, was organized and controlled.

"I think he's going to be in the lead," Neil murmured. "You've got to hand it to Marty. For such a jerk, he's very good with that dog."

As if Buster could read the clock, he accelerated hard at the last few obstacles as the crowd roared its encouragement, till he sprinted through the final gate with Marty at his side. The arena fell quiet as the board revealed Buster's latest score.

The loudspeaker crackled. "And as you can see, that excellent round by Buster and Marty Stevens takes them to the top of the Superdog! leader board."

Shannon and Barry Carpenter kept up the high

standard when they performed next. The crowd cheered their appreciation loudly as Shannon skillfully glided over the course, hardly taking a wrong step.

"Aren't they good?" Emily sighed as Shannon completed another excellent round. This time there were no disputes, just a single penalty when Shannon failed to touch the yellow painted contact zone as she bounded off the crossover table.

"Look!" said Neil, studying the scoreboard. "Shannon's still in second just behind Buster. I really don't know if Twister can keep up with that pace. Not today."

"Well, we're about to find out," Emily answered. "Here they come."

Jake pricked up his ears when he saw his new friend entering the ring below. Neil had to hold him down or he'd have jumped over the seats to join the competitors.

From the starting bell, it was as if Becky had a different dog for a partner today. Someone had left the brakes on!

Neil willed Twister to run faster, jump higher, and respond to Becky's commands more intelligently, and he found he was gripping Jake so hard that the puppy squealed in protest.

"Sorry, Jake," Neil apologized. "It's just so frustrating. I don't get why Twister is so off the mark. Do you, Emily?"

But as he spoke, a picture of Marty's gloating face came into his mind, and an idea started to form in Neil's head.

Suppose someone had messed with Twister? Surely the way he was running today couldn't be natural? But not even Marty and Gary would dream of doing that, would they? Who could be so horrible?

Becky and Twister completed the course but were way outside the time target. More than once Twister had seemed confused, and there was a moment on the seesaw when the crowd had drawn in its breath, thinking that the dog was going to lose his balance.

"A disappointing round for Becky Aslett and

Twister there. . . ." said the emcee, telling the spectators what they could see all too well on the scoreboard, "leaving them well down the field, I'm afraid.
So with just the final rounds to come tomorrow, the
new Superdog! competition leader is Buster with
Marty Stevens! Can we have a big round of applause, please?"

Ignoring the cheering in the arena, Neil and Emily
made their way down to the gate of the entrants' enclosure. Neil could see Max with a microphone in his
hand and a cameraman lurking over his shoulder,
trying to interview Becky. As Max approached her,
she brushed past him, wiping tears from her eyes,
and ran into her mom's arms, Twister following
sadly on the end of his leash.

Down in the ring, Marty, sensing victory within
his reach, broke into a cheesy, leering grin and
basked in the cheers of the crowd.

"Poor Becky," said Neil.

## CHAPTER SIX

**A**s they expected, Neil and Emily eventually found Becky back at the trailer. She was sitting on the ground under the awning with her head down, and she didn't even look up when they said hello. Twister was circling her restlessly, not sure what to make of it all. Her mom smiled a welcome at Neil and Emily from the steps, and then shook her head sadly in Becky and Twister's direction.

Neil slipped Jake's leash off, and as Neil had guessed he would, Jake went straight up to Becky and tried to lick her face. She tried to ignore him, but she couldn't keep it up for long. Half annoyed, half amused at the puppy's show of affection, Becky took his face in her hands and rubbed noses with him, sighing. "You really don't know when to leave a girl alone, do you, Jake?"

"Are you OK?" Neil asked uncertainly.

"Oh, fine," Becky snapped. "Great. Weeks of preparation and hard work down the drain. How do you *think* I am, Neil?" She hunched her shoulders and turned away again, sulking.

Neil reddened but said nothing.

"I'm sorry." Becky sniffed after a few seconds. "It's not right to take it out on you guys. You've been really good friends over the last couple of days. I'm just upset that it went wrong today. All that effort for nothing. I'm in fifth place! Fifth! I'll never make up the time now! And the worst thing is not knowing why. Perhaps Twister just isn't as good as I thought he was."

"You *know* that's not true," said Neil. "I only met Twister forty-eight hours ago, but anyone can see he's pure gold. You're a great team and you've got a brilliant future. There's got to be a reason for the way he was this afternoon. Don't you think we ought to try and see the competition vet, just in case? He must be on duty by now."

Becky looked hard at Neil. "In case of what?"

He shrugged his shoulders. "I don't know. I'm not a vet, but if you're thinking of taking part in Superdog! tomorrow, I think you ought to let him have a look."

"Suppose they say there's something really wrong?" Becky said reluctantly.

"I don't think there is. But *if* there is, you have to find out for Twister's sake, don't you?" Neil tried to sound encouraging.

"Neil's right," said Emily, offering Becky a hand up from the ground. "You know he is!"

"I suppose so," said the older girl, scrambling to her feet. "Come on, Twister, let's find out the worst!"

The vet's van and tent were not far from the ring. There were two vets on duty and, to Neil's surprise, they were both working like mad. Everyone seemed to have brought in their animals for attention.

A woman with a white coat came out of a section curtained off from the rest of the tent.

"What seems to be the problem?" the vet asked as they went behind the curtain and sat Twister on the table inside the small cubicle. The vet ran a critical eye over him and smoothed his neck hair. "Didn't I see this fellow running in Superdog! yesterday?"

Becky explained what had happened earlier that afternoon.

The vet took Twister's temperature and carefully examined his mouth, eyes, and stomach before turning back to Becky with a questioning expression on her face. "Does Twister get nervous about these sorts of things?"

Becky was puzzled. "No. He likes competing. We both do."

"And you didn't give him anything to settle him down this morning or perhaps last night?"

"No!" Neil could see that Becky was becoming indignant. Maybe she'd had a busy morning, but the vet was making Becky feel it was her fault that Twister wasn't up to snuff.

"Well, he looks as if he might have been mildly sedated to me, but if you say you haven't, then you haven't."

Becky looked as if she was going to protest, but the vet silenced her.

"I'm not going to argue," said the vet briskly. "Keep an eye on him, and if he seems no different tomorrow, bring him back to see me. There's nothing obviously wrong as far as I can see. But do remember, young lady, dogs aren't machines and you can't expect to be a winner all the time. Sometimes I think these competitions aren't always for the best. People forget it's supposed to be about taking part, not going for glory."

What she said wasn't meant to sound harsh and uncaring, but Neil could see Becky struggling to hold back a fresh batch of tears as she pulled Twister out of the vet's tent.

As Becky and Twister hurried away, Neil hung back with Emily and asked the vet, "Why did you think Twister might have had something to settle him down?"

"Are you the girl's friend?" asked the vet, gesturing after Becky. "Do you know much about dogs?" Neil briefly explained that their parents ran a boarding kennel. The vet paused and considered him for a moment.

"OK, well then, you probably know dogs have one more eyelid than us. Sometimes, if a dog's been tranquilized, you can see that extra eyelid has drawn across a bit more than usual. It's not absolutely one hundred percent, but it's a pretty reliable indicator that the dog's been sedated."

"Thank you," said Emily, nodding. "You've been very helpful. And if Twister's not better tomorrow, we'll bring him back to see you."

As they left the vet behind, Neil shook his head and exploded to Emily, "Well, that's it, then. Somebody's tampered with Twister, haven't they?"

Emily stopped and looked at her brother, eyes wide. "Do you really think so?" she said.

"Absolutely," answered Neil. "The only question is *who*? But I know who'd be top of my list."

"Marty?"

"Who else?"

"It's not going to be easy convincing Becky, though. You know what she's been like about him."

They caught up with Becky and Twister as they marched purposefully across the campsite. Neil could see that Becky was very, very angry.

"Going for glory!" she muttered. "Who does that woman think she is? It's her job to cure sick animals — not give us lectures."

"Hang on," said Neil. "We ought to talk for a minute. Where are you off to?"

"Miryam's."

"Miryam's? Why?"

"Because she saw something, that's why, and she wouldn't say all she knew. And I don't want to mess around — I want to know whether it's worth it for Twister and me to compete. It's too important." Becky stopped and looked at Neil and Emily. "You do understand, don't you? You can come along with us if you like."

Neil could see it wasn't the moment to argue. There was no way Becky was going to listen to anyone right now.

Miryam was standing by herself outside her tent, looking hot and bothered. And she didn't seem all that pleased to see them. Gypsy Rose ignored them, too, busy with exciting smells in a clump of grass nearby.

"I'm not sure we're open," Miryam grumbled, fanning herself with a show program.

"Please!" Becky implored. "I really need you to tell me a bit more about Twister. Please, Miryam, I'm really upset."

Miryam shook her head and raised her eyes to the

heavens, but she gave in and beckoned them to follow her inside. Gypsy Rose padded in behind them, jumping onto her chair and turning to study them with her one beady eye.

"Let me see him, then," she said, fixing her attention on Twister. She drew him toward her firmly but gently. The dog shook his head from side to side and tried to loosen her grip. Miryam brought her face down to his. As their eyes met, Twister stopped fidgeting at once.

Closing her eyes, Miryam hummed to herself as she ran her hands and forearms down over Twister's flanks. A familiar throaty growl began to come

from deep inside Gypsy Rose. Then suddenly, Miryam stopped humming, grimaced, and opened her eyes wide, as startled as if she'd received an electric shock.

She let Twister go and sat back on her chair, hands on knees before looking directly at Becky. "All I can tell you, my dear, is that I can feel a gap in his aura," she said.

"What do you mean? Is that bad?" said Becky, puzzled.

"How can I put it?" Miryam struggled to find the right words. "It's as if he's been invaded by some powerful force. And now he's recovering. It must have been very unpleasant for him."

"What kind of force could it have been?" said Emily eagerly, leaning forward.

Neil was still a bit skeptical and raised his eyebrows incredulously.

"Hard to say, dear," continued Miryam. "But I don't think you need to worry. His spirit's very strong, you know. He won't give in easily. He'll come back better than ever, you'll see." She got up and placed her hands on Becky's head in a way that was both kind and solemn.

Becky returned Miryam's steady gaze with watery eyes and nodded her agreement.

Then Miryam turned to Neil and Emily. "And if you all use your brains," she said, "then perhaps you'll be able to work out what it was that caused Twister the problem. And forget ghoulies and ghosties and things that go bump in the night. These things are usually much more down-to-earth. Now go on, all of you, and let me have my lunch. My word, it's three-thirty already!"

Outside, a cool breeze had sprung up to match the friends' calmer mood. Becky glanced at Neil. "I've got to put something right," she said. "Your friend Max. I was really rude to him after today's round. D'you think we could find him so I can say I'm sorry?"

They came across Max and Prince near the arena. They were watching as Mike Bishop and his assistant Paul coiled wires into silver flight cases.

Becky apologized.

Max shook his head. "It's no problem," he said. "We shouldn't have been bothering you with questions. It was pretty obvious you were upset. How's Twister now?"

Jake and Twister were having a pretend fight around their legs. Jake spilled over into a pile of wire waiting to be put away and drew an anxious "Hey, careful!" from Paul.

"I'd say he was getting better, wouldn't you?" Neil smiled.

Mike Bishop wandered over to talk to them.

"Angela told me your trailer was broken into last night," he said to Becky. "Is everything OK?"

"Yeah, it doesn't look like anything was taken," Becky answered.

Mike wiped the sweat from his forehead and came a little closer. "I don't want to point the finger," he murmured, "but you know the boy with that German shepherd you're competing against?"

"Marty Stevens?" said Neil, suddenly all ears.

"That's the one. Well, I was taking a stroll during a break in the party last night, and I ran across Marty and that creepy-looking older brother of his lurking around the campsite."

"Talk about jumping to conclusions!" interrupted Becky irritably. "They've got a trailer down there, too, you know!"

"And what were *you* doing lurking around the campsite, anyway, Mike?" asked Max cheekily.

"Look, you know what I mean." Mike laughed. "You could see they were up to mischief of some sort. It was written all over them. And if you're so smart, Max, tell me why Marty would try so hard to hide the bag of tools he was carrying? Answer me that now!"

Neil and Becky exchanged wide-eyed glances.

## CHAPTER SEVEN

There was a silence as everyone digested what Mike Bishop had just said. Neil was the first to speak. "I know you don't want to believe it, Becky," he said slowly. "I know you feel sorry for Marty. I know that he and Buster are a great team. But please just listen to me for a moment."

Neil explained to Becky about what was worrying him — how the vet had suggested Twister might have been tranquilized, and how if Marty *had* somehow broken into the trailer, he *could* have been responsible. Maybe what Miryam had picked up when she'd talked about a force invading Twister was that he'd been drugged!

Becky heard Neil out carefully and then shook her head. "You can't go around accusing people like that," she said deliberately. "There's no proof. It could just as well have been Barry Carpenter who broke in and doped Twister. He wasn't dancing with Mom *all* evening. So why aren't you accusing him? Or any of the other owners? They've got just as much to gain by Twister doing badly. What it comes down to is that you don't like Marty's face. It doesn't mean he's a criminal!"

Neil thought for a moment. What Becky was saying was right. They needed hard evidence. Maybe the tool bag Mike Bishop had seen Marty carrying would yield some secrets. But how could they ever get their hands on that?

Emily had obviously been thinking hard about the matter, too. "If it was Marty, why wasn't Shannon drugged, too?" she asked. "He's a threat to Buster as well."

"True," admitted Neil. "But maybe he *has* tried to get to Shannon, too. The Stevenses are desperate to win this thing, aren't they?" Then an idea occurred to Neil. "If we were the police, the first thing we'd do would be to inspect the scene of the crime," he said. "And we haven't really done that — not properly. There could still be a clue lying around that would tell us what happened. Becky, I think we ought to search your trailer again, really carefully, in case we've missed something."

"And there's one other thing we could do," Max chipped in. "Mike had half promised Marty's brother he'd interview the family, hadn't you, Mike? And since they're the favorites for Superdog! now, we've got the perfect excuse. Let's ask them if we can come down to their trailer and record an insert for the program about Buster. I bet they'd go for it. Who knows what we might find!"

Neil nodded enthusiastically. "I could go along with you, helping as Max's friend."

Mike Bishop made a face and said he wasn't sure Northwest Television could get dragged into an argument between the rivals for the Superdog! title. But when Max pointed out that it was Mike who'd started the discussion and wouldn't it make a terrific story if they found out that Marty had sedated Twister, he didn't take long to change his mind.

"Breaking and entering! I thought we were coming for a nice relaxing weekend in Blackpool, not to make a crime movie!" Mike Bishop moaned.

Becky's mom was sitting outside working on a tapestry when they arrived back at the trailer. She frowned when Becky told her that they wanted to search the trailer again for clues.

"Oh, Rebecca," she said. "You do pick your moments, don't you? It's been a very odd day. I just couldn't face tidying up. The place is a total mess!"

"That's great, Mrs. Aslett," said Neil. "It means you won't have destroyed any of the evidence."

"Humor him, Mom." Becky sighed. "He's got some

bee in his bonnet about Marty. This is the only way to get rid of it."

Twister curled up at Angela's feet, but Jake hurtled up the steps ahead of them and immediately started to root around under a chair. Becky quickly rescued one of her mom's slippers before it got chewed. "Come on, then, Neil. What are we looking for?" she asked.

Neil scratched his head. "I don't know," he said. "Anything an intruder might have left behind. We'll know it when we see it. Let's start in the area around Twister's basket."

Emily soon found a long hair, which Becky identified as her mom's. Neil came across an old shopping list and a ballpoint pen under a nearby bed and Becky discovered some coins.

Neil quickly became frustrated and, his imagination running away with him, he asked, "What do you think we could use to dust for fingerprints?"

Emily shook her head. "I don't think Becky's mom is going to be very pleased if we start scattering flour around, Neil."

"Don't you dare!" added Becky. "The place is enough of a mess as it is."

Finally, finding nothing of interest, they gave up and went out into the pleasantly cool afternoon. Jake pattered out of the trailer after them.

Neil found it hard to hide his disappointment. He kicked at a tuft of grass beside the trailer. Becky, who had never thought much of the plan, anyway, went to give Twister a cuddle.

"No luck?" called Becky's mom. Neil shook his head. Jake came and lay down at his feet, chewing something that he was holding in his paws. Whatever it was glinted in the low afternoon sun, catching Neil's eye.

"What have you got there, Jake?" he asked. Jake dropped the silver-and-green wrapper guiltily and Neil picked it up, thinking at first that it was the remains of a bar of chocolate. As he looked closer, he couldn't quite believe what he saw. It was too perfect. "Well, look what Jake's found!" he said. "And then tell me I wasn't right!"

It was the foil that had once been the packaging for a strip of tablets. On the foil was clearly written the name of the product: Suprapromazine.

"These are the same as the tablets Dad gave Jake before we left King Street," Neil said triumphantly. "There's your answer to why Twister was off-color this morning, Becky. It's got to be! So the only question now is, who left this inside your trailer?"

Emily took the wrapper and looked at Neil. "At least now we know what we might be looking for when we get inside Marty's place."

Just then, Max and Prince strolled into view. They brought the news that Mike Bishop had fixed it with the Stevenses. They could record an interview at their trailer this evening.

In the meantime, the friends had to rein in their impatience. They wandered up to the arena and spent an hour or two together restlessly watching the early evening displays.

A team of handlers from the government's Customs Department showed how their dogs could detect illegal drugs and contraband at ports and airports. The military police handlers put them through some slick routines, too. Neil loved to see these dogs at the peak of their condition. They were used as working dogs, but they obviously still thoroughly enjoyed life. As he watched the team of German shepherds that Buster would fit into so perfectly, he felt a pang of anxiety. What would happen to Buster if Marty *were* to blame for Twister's condition? The poor animal might lose out, big time! And a real talent might go to waste.

It was nearly seven-thirty when they went their separate ways. Emily and Becky went off together to grab something to eat while Neil and Max met up with the Northwest Television team to go and visit Marty's temporary home.

The Stevenses' trailer was large in comparison to Becky's. Together with a rusty van, their mobile living arrangements seemed to need half the field all to itself.

While Becky and her mom had joked about their own trailer being untidy, the inside of the Stevenses' was a mess. Greasy machine parts littered the kitchen table. It looked as if someone had been taking an engine apart.

"Interesting," murmured Mike Bishop, before calling to his assistant. "Paul, we'll need some light on the interior shots. You can make it look a bit *moody*, if you like." Then under his breath he added, "Though that won't be difficult."

Buster sat alertly beside the trailer, watching the activity with a keen eye. Marty's family sat around looking awkward. His brother and father were peas from the same pod, but their father had at least made an effort for the TV cameras. He wore a bright

Superdog! T-shirt and new-looking jeans. Mrs.
Stevens, who was tall and gray-haired, simply kept
out of everyone's way.

Mike Bishop lifted the news camera onto his
shoulder and took some shots of the inside of the
trailer, lingering on a variety of shiny competition
souvenirs that were attached to the walls. They were
the only items in the whole place that seemed to be
looked after.

After five minutes, he said, "Now if I can have you
all outside looking like a happy family, we'll take a
few shots of you playing with Buster. Maybe Marty
could even practice a jump with Buster or something? Then we'll get Max here to ask you a few
questions. OK? And perhaps to save our batteries, if
you've got your generator running, we could take a
feed off your power supply. Could someone show
young Neil here where to plug it in?"

Grudgingly, Marty's brother showed Neil a socket
inside the trailer. He looked sharply at Neil. "Haven't
I seen you somewhere before?" he grunted.

"I'm a friend of Max. You've probably seen me
around the grounds these last couple of days," said
Neil brightly. "We've been all over the place. And
didn't we see you at Blackpool station a couple of
days ago?"

"Yeah, maybe . . ." Marty's brother scowled and
stomped out of the trailer.

The Stevens family had become caught up in the

excitement of being in front of the cameras and no one bothered with Neil as he watched, half in, half out of the trailer. As the camera began to roll he inched back inside slowly so that he could check things out.

Every flat surface was covered in tattered dog magazines. There was nothing incriminating as far as Neil could see. He pulled casually at a cupboard door. A pile of junk cascaded from inside it, making him jump. Then to his horror, from close behind his shoulder came a gruff and sinister voice. "Well, well! Exactly what d'you think you're looking for, kid?"

It had never occurred to Neil that there might be more than four family members of the Stevens family!

He was terrified.

## CHAPTER EIGHT

**"S**orry, I should have told you there were three brothers," said Becky later on. She was standing with Neil, Emily, and Max as they waited for Sue Hooper to finish working on her stall and take them home from the arena later that evening. "It was Finn you met. You were really unlucky there, Neil. I've heard he doesn't get out of bed much. What on earth did you say?"

"I said a cable had snagged in the cupboard door and made it come open." Neil smiled ruefully. "But I'm not sure he believed me. It was just so stupid of me to assume there was no one else in the trailer."

"No harm done." Max laughed. "They were all so delighted to have their faces on TV, I'm sure they won't give it a second thought. Anyway, Finn looked completely groggy when he did come outside. I don't think he'd have noticed if you'd walked off with the family silverware."

"Family silver!" joked Becky. "He wouldn't have noticed if Buster had stood up and talked to him!" It was the first time she'd seen the funny side of anything since lunchtime.

"Ha-ha. All very amusing, but we're no closer to being able to pin anything on Marty, are we?" Neil moaned.

Emily suddenly seemed curious about exactly *where* Marty's trailer was on the campsite and what time they were due to arrive at the fairgrounds the next day.

"Quite early, I think," said Max. "There are various Superdog! events scattered throughout the day, aren't there, Becky? I think the first of them starts about ten-thirty. Mike'll want me there a good hour before that."

"Why do you want to know?" Neil asked Emily, intrigued. "If it's Dad you're worried about, he said he'd find us sometime in the late morning. He didn't think he'd get away from King Street till about nine o'clock."

"No, it wasn't that," Emily replied. "Though it'll be nice to see Dad again. I just had an idea about something, that's all. I'll tell you later."

Just then, Sue arrived, so the friends said good-bye to Becky and Twister and clambered into the car for the trip home. Jake yawned widely as he sat on Neil's lap.

"Just make sure you don't wake us up tonight," Neil warned the young puppy. "It's been a long day, and we all need some sleep." Everyone voiced their agreement.

They *did* all sleep undisturbed, and by nine o'clock on Sunday morning they were all well rested and back at the fairgrounds for the last day of the competition.

When Max and Prince had gone off to see what Mike Bishop had in store for them, Emily turned to Neil. "I've been thinking," she said. "If the Stevenses were a normal family, and they had a drug like that Suprapromazine, they wouldn't just leave it lying around, would they?"

"They're *not* a normal family, though, are they?" answered Neil. "You should have seen the inside of their trailer."

"I still think they'd put it away somewhere safe," insisted Emily, "like a bathroom cabinet, or a first-aid kit. I've got an idea how to get another look inside. I'll do it, because they know you too well now. Are you in?"

"You bet," said Neil, attaching Jake's leash to his collar. "Whatever it takes!"

Emily explained what she had in mind.

Down near the Stevenses' trailer, Neil and Emily kept themselves out of sight behind the neighboring trailers and checked for signs of life. Marty and Buster were there, all right. Marty was sitting on the trailer steps reading a comic book and humming to himself, while Buster lay at his feet. If there was anyone else at home, they were asleep. No sounds came from inside the trailer, and the Stevenses' rusty van had gone. So far, so good!

"Are you sure you're going to be OK?" Neil whispered to his sister anxiously. Neil was crouched by Jake, keeping the puppy calm.

"No problem," said Emily. "Wish me luck!"

Neil and Jake watched as Emily started her run about thirty yards from Marty's trailer. She sprinted as hard as she could on a diagonal path that would take her near the steps where Marty was sitting. They'd planned that she would fake a fall five or ten yards from him in order to get patched up inside.

Neil bit his lip as Emily suddenly tripped and fell down heavily, grazing her arm. It was far more realistic than anything Neil had dared to hope for, and even he was impressed.

As she let out a loud and genuine squeal of pain, Neil noticed the plank of wood lying in the thick grass that Emily obviously hadn't seen. Oops. Neil winced.

Emily's cries brought Marty and Buster to their feet at once.

"Are you all right?" Neil heard Marty call. He seemed flustered and unsure what to do.

Emily was slightly dazed by her fall, but in answer she feebly raised her arm. Even from where he was, Neil could see that the scrape was a nasty mix of grass stain, dirt, and blood. Marty fidgeted back and forth. He didn't look like he wanted to get involved, but obviously he couldn't leave Emily in that state.

"You'd better get that cleaned up," he muttered awkwardly. "Come on! In here!"

Neil and Jake watched Emily disappear inside the trailer with Marty, then hurried forward to try to sneak a peek inside through one of the small grimy windows.

Neil stood on a couple of bricks and peered into the gloom, motioning Jake to sit still at his feet. "Good boy," he whispered.

Inside the trailer, Marty had found Emily a cotton-ball and showed her to a dirty washbasin where a cold tap trickled just enough water to clean the scrape. When she'd done what she could, Emily asked Marty, "So, have you got a bandage?"

Neil observed Emily watching Marty like a hawk as he opened a cupboard door, hunting around inside for something that would do. *That's the kind of place we're looking for,* thought Neil. *Yes!* A glint of silver and green flashed in the light coming through the window.

Emily clutched hold of the table. "I don't feel very well," she said. "Actually, I feel a bit faint. Can you get me a glass of water?"

Neil could see Marty hesitating. The last thing he'd want with the next round of Superdog! less than an hour away was to have someone fainting on him. He went to get the water, leaving her on her own. In the few seconds his back was turned, Emily carefully reached into the cupboard, snatched the green-and-silver foil, and stuffed it into her jeans pocket.

Neil heard Emily saying she had to leave, and he rushed back under cover with Jake.

Emily joined him seconds later, and they waited until they were well clear of the trailer before they dared to look at exactly what it was Emily had stolen from the Stevenses' medicine chest. When they read the name Suprapromazine on the packet, Neil couldn't resist punching the air and letting out a "Yes!" of triumph.

"Emily, that was amazing!" said Neil. "Good job!" Jake recognized the wrapping and tried to snatch it from Emily's hand.

"Oh, no, Jake, please don't eat the evidence!" said Emily proudly. "Not after all that!" Then she rubbed her arm. "Ow, my arm really *does* hurt!"

Emily, Neil, and Jake found Becky and Twister on a piece of open ground behind the arena, practicing their Frisbee skills for the next event. They could see at a glance that Twister was back to his old lively and playful self.

"So we've nailed Marty," crowed Neil, when they'd told an astonished Becky what had happened. "What do we do now?"

"Well, hang on a minute," said Becky. "I agree it's not looking good for the Stevens family, but it's not exactly in the bag, is it? For a start, we don't *know* that Twister was definitely under the influence of that Supra stuff, we only *think* he was. Second, you can't be sure whether Marty's to blame or someone else in his family. And, anyway, if you used the drug to keep Jake calm, why can't they keep some for Buster? It could all be a complete coincidence!"

As she spoke, Becky was pacing up and down on the grass. "I can't believe it was really Marty. I ran into him as I was walking Twister last night and, in his own funny way, he seemed genuinely sorry Twister had been feeling bad. One moment I'm sure you're right, Neil, and the next I'm sure you're not. I can't figure it out at all!"

"It's really odd, you know," added Emily. "Marty was so nice when I hurt myself. I don't think he'd really want to do anybody harm. It's just like he doesn't know how to get along with people."

"Not you, too!" said Neil, dismayed. "Why do you both keep defending him?" It was so frustrating. Every time Neil thought they were getting close to solving the mystery, it seemed they took several steps backward.

"No offense, guys," said Becky suddenly, trying to brush the intrigue out of her mind, "but Twister and I have got to get ready for the Frisbee. We'll have to talk about this later."

"Is there any point in carrying on, anyway?" said Neil, suddenly downcast.

Becky's eyes flashed. "You bet. You wouldn't want us to give up, would you? There's the Frisbee, the swimming, and the agility to come. That's three chances to show we're the best, even if Twister doesn't get to be Superdog. If someone has been trying to tamper with Twister, the last thing we'd want would be to let them think they had us beat."

Canine Frisbee fascinated Neil. He'd messed around throwing a Frisbee with Sam a few times in the past, but, although Sam's catching wasn't bad, Neil had never quite mastered the art of making the piece of plastic go where he wanted it to. The Frisbee always had a mind of its own.

This competition wasn't just about catching, though, it was freestyle. Each pair had ninety seconds to put together a program that was as fun and clever as they could make it. And, if they wanted, they could do it to music, though Neil wasn't too sure his dad would have liked that!

*"What will they think of next!"* he could imagine

him saying. *"They'll be dressing up the dogs soon!"*
Bob Parker was always concerned about treating
dogs properly as dogs, not as second-rate humans.

The teams were still running in reverse order,
with those placed last running first, so it was an
hour before Becky and Twister took center stage.
Unlike all the other competitors, they didn't use a
piece of predictable pop music. It was something
classical, with lots of crashing cymbals and loud
staccato bursts of drums. Neil thought it sounded
like fireworks, and Twister's catches of the Frisbee
were very smooth.

"That is *so* clever!" Emily said with admiration. "They don't ever seem to mess up."

"They must have practiced for hours," agreed Neil. "I wouldn't have the patience!"

In the time allowed, using a half dozen Frisbees of different colors, Becky must have thrown as many as twenty times. Her throws came from behind her back, between her legs, and over her shoulder, and Twister only missed three of them!

Twister seemed able to remember exactly what was going to happen next, and on a couple of occasions caught Frisbees that seemed way out of reach, twisting and arching his back as if gravity didn't exist. When they'd finished, everyone in the arena stood and roared with applause.

"That was fantastic!" Neil shouted, leaping to his feet and suddenly feeling much better. "That showed them! There's only one Superdog, and his name's Twister!"

"Sit down, Neil," said Emily, embarrassed. "It sounds as if you need something to calm *you* down!"

Afterward, no one in the Frisbee competition could better their score. Shannon and Buster both made decent attempts at entertaining the crowd but had lost ground at the top of the leader board. When all the teams had finished their routines, Becky and Twister had narrowed the gap and moved up one level into fourth place.

"That's a bit of a bummer," said Neil, fishing Jake's

water bowl and a bottle of water from his backpack.
"They're still so far behind Buster and Shannon.
They'll never win from where they are now!"

"Well, it was still excellent," Emily replied as the
spectators began to leave their seats. "They were certainly better than the other competitors. Perhaps,
one day, it'll be you and Neil, Jake. What d'you
think?" Jake shook himself and barked.

"Do I take that as a 'yes' or a 'no'?" Neil smiled.

"Oh, look, there's Dad," said Emily, waving at the
large, bearded man. "Let's go and grab him."

"Hi, Dad! Did you see any of that?" asked Neil enthusiastically after they'd made their way over the
seats.

"What, the Frisbee? Yes, I think I saw most of it.
That girl with the mongrel was very good, wasn't
she?" Bob Parker grinned. He greeted Jake affectionately and gathered him up in his powerful arms.

"That's Becky," said Emily proudly. "She's a friend
of ours. You'll probably meet her in a minute."

"What *have* you done to your arm, Emily?" Bob
asked anxiously. "You look as if you've been in a
war!"

"Well, a lot's happened since we've been in Blackpool," answered Neil. And he went on to tell his dad
what had taken place since Thursday night.

While Neil was telling their story, Becky and
Twister arrived and were introduced to Bob. When
he'd heard everything, Bob shook his head and

sighed. "The things people do, and the risks they take with their animals as well as themselves!" he said. "It makes my blood boil." Then he turned and looked Becky straight in the eye. "It's a shame to leave it there, isn't it? Are you going to take things further?" he asked.

She returned his gaze steadily. "I keep thinking about it," she said. "We've got to know the whole truth, don't we? Or whoever it is that's responsible might do something worse the next time!"

"But we're running out of time," said Neil, combing his fingers through his hair in growing desperation. "And we're running out of ideas. With every minute that passes, Marty's more likely to get away with it and win Superdog!"

## CHAPTER NINE

Neil and Emily exchanged anxious glances with Becky. For the moment, none of them knew what to do next.

"You say the drug might have been given to Twister on Friday evening?" Bob checked with Becky. She nodded. "The way I see it, then, what you need to find out," he continued, "is whether a blood test would still show traces of the Suprapromazine thirty-six hours later. You ought to find that vet you saw yesterday and see what the chances are."

"What are we waiting for?" said Emily.

"Well, I don't know about you guys," said Becky, "but I'm starving. Twister and I start the swimming at one o'clock, and he needs to be fed, watered, and rested by then, so we're not going to be much help."

"Why don't Emily and I try to find out about the blood test," Neil offered. "I just can't bear to sit around doing nothing. Will you come with us, Dad?"

They gave Jake some more water to stop him from dehydrating in the hot sun, grabbed a burger from a nearby stand, then Neil, Emily, and Bob set out to find the vet.

The vet's tent was quieter than the previous day, though the woman who'd examined Twister was nowhere in sight. The other vet was immersed in what looked like a long conversation with the worried owner of a rather lame golden retriever. A veterinary nurse was sitting on the edge of a table, swinging her legs and looking a bit bored.

The nurse didn't know where the vet was. "She's gone off somewhere to see someone, I think," she said vaguely.

When they came back to have another look after twenty frustrating minutes, the vet still wasn't there.

"She did come back," simpered the nurse, "but she's gone off again. I think she's with the psychic lady."

Bob raised an eyebrow, and Neil found himself defending Miryam. "She's quite sensible really, Dad."

"It's not her I'm worried about. What kind of vet has to check her diagnosis with a psychic?"

"I really want to see the swimming," said Emily as the Parkers marched away from the arena down to Miryam's tent.

"There's plenty of time," Neil replied. "We'll only be a few minutes talking to the vet. Twister's swimming fourth from last."

When they arrived at Miryam's tent, they peered in and found her talking to the vet.

"I'm sure Gypsy Rose will be fine," the vet said to Miryam. "Just don't forget that ointment for her eye three times a day. However much you hate it!" she added severely, wagging her finger at Rose.

Miryam caught Neil's curious look.

"Well, the eye patch isn't just for show, you know," she said. "Poor Gypsy's had an eye infection for weeks. But the patch does look good on the signboard." And she winked at Neil and said good-bye.

As they walked away from Miryam, the vet said, "You were with that young woman and her mongrel yesterday, weren't you?"

"Becky and Twister," Neil reminded her.

"That's right. So what can I do for you?"

Neil filled her in on the details of what had happened since yesterday, without mentioning Marty or his family. The vet stopped and looked gravely at them.

"Well, given what you say, and from what I saw, I'm quite sure you're right that someone's been interfering with Twister. And yes, it's quite likely that a blood test would still show traces of Suprapromazine."

"So if we bring Twister along after the swimming event, you'll take a blood sample?" asked Neil eagerly.

The vet looked at him hard. "Yes, if that's what you want. But just think it through for a moment. What are you going to do then? All it proves is that *someone* interfered with Twister, not that any particular person did. And I won't get an answer from the laboratory till Wednesday at the earliest, when everyone will be long gone from here. Is it worth it?"

As they left the vet and strolled back toward the ring, Neil was fuming. "I told you. Marty's going to get away with it," he exploded.

"Sadly, I'm afraid cheaters sometimes *do* get away with their crimes," his dad replied, putting an arm around Neil. "Though I'm not sure Marty's off the hook just yet."

"How come?" asked Neil.

"Well, you could always try confronting him with what you know."

As Neil thought about his dad's last comment, they arrived back at the arena in the nick of time to see the swimming.

Kayleigh, the dog just behind Twister, in fifth place overall, was swimming as they took their seats, but her performance didn't suggest she was likely to improve her position.

Inside the ring, the organizers had assembled a

large, circular swimming tank. There was a walkway
around it and a ramp so that the dogs could enter
the water easily. For this fourth Superdog! event, the
dog simply had to complete three laps of the pool.
The faster he could swim, the more points he scored.
His partner walked in front, encouraging and giving
commands. On the last lap, the dog had to collect a
wooden baton from the poolside and carry it "home"
to a predetermined point.

In the events so far, Neil hadn't really taken in
just how strong Twister was, but when it was his
turn in the pool, his powerful legs carried him
quickly through the water.

"Look at him go!" he said excitedly. "He's much
quicker than Kayleigh. If the other dogs are like her,
Twister's bound to make up some more places!"

Bob nodded approvingly. "Twister's a great dog, for
sure. And what's really impressive is his stamina.
He's getting quicker over the last lap, if anything."

Twister's time was the fastest yet, and Neil prayed
that none of the three dogs who swam afterward
would match it. Becky's dog had done brilliantly
coming back in the competition after his disastrous
second round.

Another Border collie, who was in third place,
swam terribly, lost several points, but was still just
far enough ahead of Twister to stay in third. Shannon, however, performed admirably as expected and

took the lead. The pressure was now on Marty's dog to reclaim the top spot.

Everything was going well for Buster, until the last lap when Marty had to steer him in to get the baton. After completing the laps in the fastest time so far, for once Buster didn't seem to be paying attention, and Marty was working like mad to get him to respond. The walkway had become wet from all the splashes of the other competitors, and, suddenly, Marty's left foot slipped from under him. For a second, he balanced hopelessly on his other foot before

he keeled over and crashed down to join Buster in
the water.

Emily's hand went to her mouth as the whole audience teetered between laughter and sympathy at
Marty's plight. "Poor Marty!"

"Poor Marty?" exclaimed Neil. "You've got to be
joking!"

"Getting the least he deserves, by the look of it!"
said Bob, stifling a chuckle.

Jake, ears pricked, with his feet on the seat in
front, was barking furiously as if he, too, thought it
very funny.

Marty climbed out awkwardly, though it seemed
as if only his pride was really hurt. Buster eventually kept on and picked up the baton before gallantly
swimming on to the finish. Neil hoped that Marty
would now finally lose the lead and give Becky a better chance of catching up.

When the final positions were posted on the scoreboard, Marty and Buster were in second place.

"At least Shannon's in the lead, now," said Emily,
looking disappointed. "That's some consolation!"

Neil scowled. "Hardly!"

Superdog! was rapidly coming to its climax. The very
moment the swimming was finished, a swarm of officials rushed into the arena to set up the last event of
the competition — the agility contest.

The Parkers all met up with Becky and Twister outside the enclosure just before three o'clock.

"You're a champion swimmer, Twister," said Emily, smoothing his forehead.

"The highest score of the round!" added Neil.

"Yeah, wasn't he great?" said Becky. "I don't think I've ever seen him swim that fast before. He knows he's got to make up for yesterday."

"Twister is up to fourth now. I really think you still have a chance, you know," said Neil.

Becky shook her head. "Not unless both Shannon and Buster break a leg. Realistically, it'll still need a miracle."

Neil laughed wickedly. "Marty might be coming down with pneumonia this very minute."

Becky grinned. "I know. Wasn't that fall of his *awful*? In front of all those people. I'd have died!"

"It's a shame Buster had to suffer, though. He's such a great dog," said Neil's dad. "Hey, look! Isn't that him?"

Marty and Buster were hovering anxiously nearby. For a few seconds, it looked as if Marty badly wanted to say something to Becky, but then at the last moment, embarrassed by the fact that all her friends were there laughing, he pulled away, apparently changing his mind.

"Are you OK, Marty?" Becky called out as he retreated.

"Yeah, fine," he said weakly over his shoulder. "Fine."

"You'd almost have thought that young man wanted to confess to something, wouldn't you?" said Bob Parker, looking meaningfully at Neil.

The last event gave the teams a chance to clock up as many points as they could in two minutes. Event officials had marked out five red obstacles worth one point each, and five in other colors, each worth a different number of points. You had to keep clearing a red obstacle, followed by a colored one, until the whole field was cleared. Each handler was under real pressure to guess their best route and to judge the time accurately. Once again, the competitors were to run in reverse order, so Shannon, who was currently in the lead, would have to run last.

"I feel really nervous," said Neil as he looked down on the complicated-looking course. "Goodness knows how Becky's feeling."

As they waited for Twister's turn, the tension mounted, each competitor adding to the overall atmosphere until, fourth from last, Becky and Twister took to the ring.

When the bell sounded, there was no sensation of panic or rush from either girl or dog. It was as if the two of them floated over, around, and under the obstacles. Becky was ice-cool, mentally ticking off the items one by one. They were far, far ahead of

everyone else so far. What counted was to make sure that each obstacle was cleared properly, so that every score counted.

The blue obstacle was a double-spread jump for five points. Twister pinned back his ears and sailed clear. Then there was a tight turn into the seesaw, counting for six. His feet moved perfectly in and out of the obstacle. In two strides, Twister was over a red obstacle, then at the weaving poles — the black and hardest test, counting for seven points. There were three or four seconds remaining — no more — as he went into the slalom.

Neil thought it impossible that the bell for the two

minutes wouldn't beat Twister to the finish, but he was smoothly in and out of the last gates and sprinting for home effortlessly, to a deafening shout of approval from the crowd as Becky danced for joy. It was as near a perfect round as Neil could imagine. Twister was in the provisional top spot — but with three teams still to score points.

"There's no doubt. They've got real talent," said Bob. "It still amazes me when I see someone that natural with their animal as Becky."

"But has she done enough?" asked Emily anxiously.

"It doesn't matter in the end," said her dad. "What matters is being the best you can be."

The friends sank back into their seats exhausted. They'd been over and under every obstacle with Twister. After an ordinary performance from the team in third place, Twister stayed on top. Already, they were guaranteed a bronze medal. Neil and Emily were thrilled for Twister and Becky but could they do any better?

The ten minutes of truth were yet to come.

In all honesty, if Becky and Twister hadn't been so fantastic just before, Neil would have said that Buster was magnificent. His strength and quickness on the turn were lovely to watch and, like Twister, he had the ability to eat up the ground. It didn't once look as if he was straining. After he'd finished his round to generous applause, the friends waited the few seconds for his score to show on the board. Mike Bishop's camera was in close on Marty and Buster, waiting to capture their reactions.

Buster had moved back up to first place.

Neil covered his head with his hands. "That's it! Becky and Twister are out of it. Ugh, I can't believe it. I really thought that Marty would foul it up at the last minute."

"It's not over yet," said his dad. "You can never be sure!"

Neil felt sick at the thought that Buster would win the Superdog! competition. It wasn't right! Now only Shannon could prevent Marty's final and total triumph.

Neil prayed that she could.

## CHAPTER TEN

As Barry Carpenter and Shannon the Border collie ran out into the packed Superdog! arena, Neil and Emily cheered for them as long and loudly as they had for anything all weekend.

But, hard though Shannon tried, the sparkle that was in her performance on the first two days just *wasn't* there. Barry Carpenter himself seemed a bit off the pace, and it wasn't until the final few high-scoring obstacles that there seemed any sense of urgency about the team. The crowd cheered them on, knowing it must still be incredibly close between Shannon and Buster.

Shannon was over the double spread cleanly, neatly around to the seesaw, and then on to the weaving poles. But her balance wasn't quite right, and to a groan from the spectators she swerved to the wrong side of one of the gates. Neil held his head in his hands. Seven points lost, at the final, crucial moment.

"It must be so tight," said Bob excitedly.

"They haven't done it," said Neil, making frantic calculations in his head. "I don't think Shannon's scored enough points."

Emily crossed her fingers superstitiously.

Neil could see Becky and Twister down near the scoreboard with some of the other competitors, waiting anxiously for the final, overall standings to flash up.

The electronic scoreboard remained agonizingly blank.

Suddenly, the loudspeaker came to life, and simultaneously an animated flash of colorful graphics paraded across the board heralding the final results. One by one the team names appeared, covering the positions up to fourth place.

The crowd cheered as each name appeared.

"The results of the first ever Superdog! competition are . . ." proclaimed the voice from the loudspeaker.

Neil shuddered in nervous excitement.

"In third place . . ." the voice paused, ". . . is Twister, and his partner, Miss Becky Aslett!"

Thunderous applause echoed around the arena as the crowd remembered the great entertainment they'd enjoyed.

"In second place . . ." the announcer continued.

Neil bit his nails at the frustratingly long pause that followed. *Get on with it!* he thought.

". . . is Shannon, trained by Mr. Barry Carpenter."

Neil's head dropped, and next to him he heard Emily groan.

The announcer's voice then seemed to rise an octave as he said, "And by the narrowest of margins, this year's Superdog is Buster, trained by his owner, Marty Stevens!"

The arena erupted in applause.

Neil glanced down at the enclosure. He'd expected to see Marty overjoyed, jumping up and down, relishing his moment of glory, but the winning owner seemed subdued. Coming in first, in the end, hadn't brought him any happiness.

Neil put his hands in his pocket and felt the scratch of the foil containing the Suprapromazine they'd discovered in Marty's trailer. Suddenly, his dad's words came back to him. . . . *"You'd almost have thought that young man wanted to confess to something. . . ."*

"Just a minute," he said to Emily and his dad. "This might be my last chance to do something about Marty."

"Do you want us to come with you?" asked Bob.

"No. The fewer people, the better, I think," answered Neil.

The presentation of the medals and prizes by Max

wasn't due to begin for several minutes, until the course officials had finished erecting the ceremonial platform, so Neil knew he only had a short time to act.

The guard at the enclosure knew Neil by now and let him in without question. Neil made straight for Marty, anxious to get to him before any of the rest of the Stevens family showed up.

"Hold on, Marty, I'd like a word with you." Neil's voice was quiet but firm.

"Oh? And why would I want to talk to you?" Marty replied petulantly.

"Is this a good enough reason?" said Neil, producing the green-and-silver foil from his pocket, so that only Marty could see it.

As he realized what Neil was holding in his hand, Marty's eyes narrowed and the color drained from his face.

Neil waved at Becky to join them. She'd seen Neil arrive in the enclosure, and she left Twister on his leash with her mom and ran to their side.

"We know," said Neil simply, dangling the foil from his fingers.

Marty scrunched up his eyes. They looked watery. He hung his head. "I didn't want to do it. I told Gary it was wrong."

"*What* was wrong?" said Becky softly.

"Him going into your trailer. Feeding your dog the pills. I was worried sick they might kill him."

"You didn't stop him, though." Becky's voice trembled. "You didn't say anything."

"It wasn't your idea, then?" pushed Neil. "It was your brother's, is that what you're telling us?"

"What do you think I am?" Marty was genuinely angry. "I'm not like them, you know. It's just about the money for them. But I really care about the dogs. Buster means everything to me."

"Like Twister means to me." Becky's words were cutting.

Marty pushed a dirty fist across his eyes, wiping away his tears of shame. He was a picture of misery. Buster could see his partner was distressed, and he nuzzled into Marty's side. By instinct, Marty's hand at once went down to stroke him.

Seeing Buster's good heart and Marty's affection for him, Becky's own eyes filled. She said nothing for a moment, allowing Marty to think about what had happened. Finally, she spoke. "OK, Neil, let's leave it there. I think Marty's learned his lesson, don't you?"

But Neil's sense of right and wrong wouldn't let it rest. "No, I'm sorry, Becky. Marty can't just walk away from this," he insisted. "You've got to make things right, Marty, for Becky's sake, and for your own sake, too. Otherwise you're going to have to go up there and take a prize you won by cheating, aren't you? How could you live with that? How could you ever enjoy competing with Buster again?"

Marty looked at them in horror. "What do I have to do?" he asked.

Neil's answer was interrupted by a terrible commotion coming from the arena. Neil and Becky swiveled around and strained to peer through the crowd to see what was causing the disturbance.

In a gap between the people, Neil caught sight of a familiar black-and-white form dodging in and out of the spectators. "Oh, no!" he cried. "It's Jake. He's on the loose again. How on earth did that happen?"

"No excuse this time," chuckled Becky. "Drug-free, a good night's sleep, and he's still a wanderer!"

Most of the crowd, as well as the TV cameras, were focused on Jake. Some of them were cheering as Jake continued a headlong course from the stands toward the Superdog! awards platform. As Neil and Becky looked on, a competition official dived heroically for Jake's leash and rounded him up.

A red-faced Neil sheepishly rushed forward to get him.

When Neil went back with Jake to find Becky, Marty had gone.

"He just took off," she said, shrugging her shoulders. "I don't have a clue where."

"Well, you'd better go and get your prize," Neil replied, his ears still tipped with pink. "You both deserve it. No one could have done any better under the circumstances."

"Thanks, Neil," said Becky. "You've all been so kind. I don't know what we'd have done without you."

"Well, there's nothing else we can do now," said Neil, suddenly deflated. "I'll take my crazy mutt back to the rest of my family, and we'll find you after the presentation."

When Neil and Jake rejoined Bob and Emily, they were the center of attention. It felt as if everyone in the stands was turning to point and giggle.

Emily grinned nervously at Neil's glare. "He just . . . slipped away from me. Sorry!"

"It's back to school for you tomorrow," said Bob, wagging his finger at Jake. "What have they been doing to you since you've been away?"

An announcement from the loudspeaker declared it time for the Superdog! presentation. The president of the show was there, and Max and Prince took their places on the platform. Mike Bishop was lurking beneath and around them, camera rolling, while the competing teams, their families, and supporters watched from the floor of the arena. All the Stevens family had gathered, managing to look threatening and sinister even on a sunny Sunday afternoon.

The president introduced Max and Prince, and moments later Twister's and Becky's names were called out to take their prize for third place. They went up to shake hands with Max and get a beauti-

fully sculpted glass statuette of a Border collie leaping into the air. As she took it, the crowd applauded
wildly, and Becky clapped her hands above her head
in acknowledgment.

Then Neil, Emily, Bob, and Jake watched as Barry
Carpenter and Shannon were called to collect their
second prize.

Suddenly, before they approached the platform,
Marty appeared on the stage, brandishing something in his hand and gesticulating wildly.

"What's going on?" whispered Emily.

"I wonder . . ." answered an astonished Neil.

Neil could hear snatches of confused conversation

through the microphone. The Stevens family growled at one another, restless and puzzled. What had gotten into their boy?

The president was looking flustered, his silver mustache quivering, his face becoming more flushed by the second. Another official rushed to his side. Neil could see a lot of arm-waving going on.

Then Marty suddenly stalked off, leaving the two men shrugging their shoulders.

Eventually, and seemingly very reluctantly, the president came back to the microphone, shaking his head. He coughed and, sounding very embarrassed, said, "Ladies and gentlemen, owing to the late withdrawal of Buster and Marty Stevens from the competition in . . . um . . . rather unprecedented fashion, I have great pleasure in announcing this year's Superdog is Shannon, owned and trained by Barry Carpenter! Would they like to come up and receive their prize, please?"

Neil could see that Barry Carpenter couldn't quite believe his luck. What the president had said took a few moments to sink in, but then a broad grin spread across Barry's face, and he and Shannon went up to take the crowd's applause, their heads held high.

"Wow!" gasped Emily. "Marty confessed!"

"Well done, Neil and Emily!" said Bob. "I bet that's your doing!"

Jake woofed loudly and wagged his tail.

"Yes, it is! You did your part, too!" Bob smiled.

"So Becky and Twister are second!" Emily said. "That's awesome!"

"That's *nearly* awesome," added Neil. "*Completely* awesome would have been a win for Twister."

Fifteen minutes later, all the friends were laughing together again by Northwest Television's van as Mike Bishop and Paul the assistant packed up their equipment.

"What did Marty say?" Neil asked Max.

"A jumble of things, but nothing made much sense. Something about the registration form not having been filled in properly, and the check for the registration fee would bounce, anyway. He said he hadn't won it fair and square, and that he didn't want the prize."

"Everyone must have been shocked!" said Neil.

"He didn't leave them much choice," added Mike Bishop. "What can you do if someone says they're not interested in winning anymore?"

"It was very brave of Marty," said Becky. "I hate to think what his family will have to say."

"It's Buster I'm worried about," Neil observed. "I hope Marty's able to look after him. And it's *still* not fair to you and Twister."

Twister brushed the ground with his tail and bared his teeth in what seemed very much like a grin.

"There's always next year." Becky was cheerful

now. She clutched her new *second* prize tightly — a silver plaque embossed with the Superdog! logo. "At least Shannon won it on merit — I don't mind that so much. And we'll be even better then, won't we?"

"Though you might have some competition!" said Mike Bishop, looking at Jake. "We've got some fantastic material on tape of Jake's exploits in the arena just then. I wouldn't be at all surprised if he makes the ten o'clock news — if we can get to Manchester in time! It's really *very* funny!"

"What do you think, Jake?" Neil bent to ruffle the puppy's ears. "Are you a Superdog in the making?"

Jake barked his agreement loudly.

Neil had absolutely no doubt. Give him a year or two, and Twister and Shannon would have no chance! No chance at all!